BALLAD OF DESCENT

Writings from an Unbound Europe

■ □ ■ □ ■

MARTIN VOPĚNKA

BALLAD OF DESCENT

Translated by Anna Bryson

With a Foreword by Karen von Kunes

NORTHWESTERN UNIVERSITY PRESS

EVANSTON, ILLINOIS

Northwestern University Press
Evanston, Illinois 60208-4210

First published in Czech as *Balada o sestupu,* Rozmluvy, Prague, 1992.
English translation published 1995 by arrangement with
Martin Vopěnka. Copyright © 1995 by Northwestern University Press.

Printed in the United States of America

Library of Congress Cataloging-in-Publication Data

Vopěnka, Martin, 1963–
    [Balada o sestupu. English]
    Ballad of descent / Martin Vopěnka ; translated by Anna Bryson ;
with a foreword by Karen von Kunes.
      p. cm. — (Writings from an unbound Europe)
    ISBN 0-8101-1252-3. — ISBN 0-8101-1253-1 (pbk.)
    I. Bryson, Anna. II. Title. III. Series.
PG5039.32.06413   1995
891.8'635—dc20   95-8674
                               CIP

■ □ ■ □ ■

CONTENTS

FOREWORD BY
KAREN VON KUNES

IN LITERARY CRITICISM CZECH LITERATURE HAS BEEN BOTH honored and dismissed. If some of the best Czech writers have failed to influence world literature it is because they failed to transform the struggle pertinent to Czechs into a drama of universal significance. Karel Čapek, Milan Kundera, Václav Havel and Josef Škvorecký have, without doubt, succeeded; Bohumil Hrabal and Vladimír Páral, on the other hand, are largely inaccessible, except to a Czech—and, to some extent, European—readership. Since the political upheavals in Eastern Europe, however, unknown writers have been ascendant on the Czech literary scene. One of them, Martin Vopěnka, stands out as a writer with a new voice in 1989 postrevolutionary literature.

Claiming no affinity to any literary group, Vopěnka is unique in his literary approach: reminiscent of absurdist traditions, yet preserving clarity and short-sentence structure. The older generation of Czech Jews, such as Ivan Klíma and Arnošt Lustig, were survivors of concentration camps, and they traditionally portrayed Jews as victims of the Nazi period. Vopěnka, a Czech Jew from Prague, deals instead with existentialist issues of present-day Eastern Europe. Born in 1963, Vopěnka is a product of communist society, "freed" from his ethnic links and traditions. But this freedom only means more hardship for him; he must seek his identity and his roots in the rootless new order of Eastern Europe.

In this search, Vopěnka turns to Kafka as his inspirational father. As does Kafka, he revives the irrational in man, turning the mystifying and inexplicable into reality. His educational background is atypical for a postmodernist writer; possessing degrees in mathematics and nuclear physics, Vopěnka abandoned science to pursue a literary career. By the time he published his first two works in 1989, *Kameny z hor* (Rocks from the Mountains) and *Balada o sestupu* (Ballad of Descent), his name had been circulating in the Prague literary journals *Tvar, Iniciály, Souvislosti,* and *Literární noviny.* It is perhaps his science-oriented mind that makes Vopěnka a seemingly humorless absurdist. Unlike Dürrenmatt's, Ionesco's, or even Kafka's eloquent sense for absurd humor, Vopěnka's subtle sense of humor is less present and less evident. But his ability to mix reality and imagination is abundant; symbolism and metaphors intervene with reality from the first pages of the book. In its form and plot, *Ballad of Descent* is a continuation of *Kameny z hor,* a booklet of lyric prose resembling a diary.

The story of *Ballad of Descent* begins with two young men leaving Prague on Christmas Day for "that other Country." Although their destination is the mountains, clearly their real search is for their own identity. People in the narrator's country have all become alike; losing their individual values in their sameness, they have become mindless, Kafkaesque products of a totalitarian regime. Unlike the castle in Kafka's novel, however, "that other Country" can be entered, and unlike the castle in Klíma's play, it can also be left. The two men, the story narrator Martin—obviously the author himself—and his friend Tomas, are led in and out by two mysterious men, Romu and Remu. In "that other Country" they become guests of a high-school professor, and Martin is "resurrected" through his spiritual and physical love for the professor's daughter Livia. Participating in "that other Country's" people's revolt, Martin loses Livia in the crowd. The protesters are beaten by the police, and subsequently, Martin is haunted by guilt for not having saved Livia's life.

The symbolic meaning of *Ballad of Descent* outweighs its story: it is the idea, not the action or the place, that is significant. The author does not reveal the name of "that other Country"; neither does he reveal its ideological tendencies, or the year in which the story has taken place. It is the author's interpretation of the individual being lost in a world of chaos and futility that makes this book universal. "That other Country" represents a merciless machine of oppressive regulations that deprives people of all hope. While the reader may understand "that other Country" as a metaphor for Romania, he also may see it as a response to current issues in former East European countries, including Serbia-Croatia-Bosnia, and on a larger scale, countries like Rwanda and Haiti. Vopěnka's message is evident: each individual, conscious of his own guilts, should accept his responsibility to make the world better.

Martin Vopěnka's novel was published by the Prague-based house Rozmluvy (formerly located in Surrey, England) and was serialized for Czech radio. Joseph Brodsky, a Russian émigré writer now living in the United States, recently stated that Czechs remain "a driving force behind civilized society;" that Vopěnka's literature is made accessible to a mass audience is proof of this commitment.

WITHOUT DIVINE OMENS

I

IT WAS THE TWENTY-FIFTH OF DECEMBER, HALF PAST SIX IN the morning, and at last I caught sight of Tomas's blond hair. At that moment there were only a few people standing around in the station concourse, and they kept a kind of pious silence. Tomas's steps were unsteady, drowsy. As if they reflected my inner state. I chose to turn my head away.

We looked at each other. "I wonder if you remember," I drew in breath for the well-prepared line, "the last time we were together on Christmas morning?" To be honest, just then I couldn't imagine anything worse than leaving my home and bed on Christmas morning. Everywhere desolation and darkness: cold, mud, ice. And behind every window happy children were sleeping, just as on that last occasion, and the air was scented with Christmas cake. But today we were traveling to that other Country, while that time . . . that time it had just been foolery. And it isn't decent to get up on Christmas morning out of foolery. "You realize, Tomas, we went off to the gym on Christmas morning."

We stood right at the back—by the entrance to the platform. Gloomy thoughts were running through our heads, and I said, "That girl looks like she's had a reckless night in some dorm," and everything inside me clenched tight as I imagined the scene. But there were more important matters:

plastic sheets for snow bivouacs, sleeping bags, cross-country ski poles, snowshoes. Considering the hour just passing we felt rather out of place.

And then we set off toward the train. It was waiting— taciturn and cold. Most of the doors were wide open, letting the fluorescent light fall into desolate interiors. One after the other we swung ourselves up on the footboards and the car gave a hollow shudder.

It was the end of another Christmas.

II

I was awakened by unbearable heat as the train hurtled incessantly forward. What existed was the day, and stinking clothes sticking to moist skin, and Tomas still sleeping, a drop of sweat running down his face, the hot stagnant air, the curtain, the faded lamp bereft of meaning . . . and it was all rushing forward. And there were rails rattling with the impact of wheels and a chill wind hurtling backward behind the windows.

Tomas's face always wore a look of innocence. The kind of innocence that could become a weapon. But now, as he slept, it testified to the inner calm that comes after some great tension, and this awoke my trust. So I got up and went out— slightly unsteady from the light and from consciousness of how ordinary a thing it was to be going to that other Country.

At the end of the corridor the doors clicked open. A woman emerged and with her a memory of Martina. It was hard to say how this woman resembled her. What recalled Martina in her was actually what was missing in Martina. Among other things: this woman was distinctly middle-aged while Martina was still only a girl, although definitely quite a lot older than I.

In fact I used to see her only from a distance. That Amazon and she-wolf. In her face I used to read her former beauty, which must have been still greater than her present beauty, itself not small. She had long, raven hair combed down her back and she was sharply intelligent—her forehead high and her figure slim but full. Had she lived in an age before history she would have been depicted as a goddess, mother of the tribe and giver of life, but she was more; she carried within herself the seed of a line that would never be born into this world. Passed unregarded, or never discovered, even perhaps undiscoverable, she courageously bore her too intelligent beauty and her peculiar fate: to be touched by the hand of God in the cradle, once and never again. And I felt that her smile was turning a little sour, after all, as well as her hips. I sensed that this sourness had entered the lupine breasts from which fair milk had never gushed to feed sons who would later have founded the new Rome; they never will because our World is simply too old for great legends . . . and this too is the reason why her womb will turn bitter and sour forever.

Yes, this is the way she would have looked if she had lost everything that had made her herself. I considered the thought and set the memory free through the open window, into the wind.

I went back to our compartment. Tomas was no longer asleep. When I entered he stretched sleepily, slid his legs down from the bench and remained in the same position. I have to admit that he looked masculine even though he didn't need to shave and the fair hair was receding from his forehead. He possessed a certain guilelessness and a certain swagger, and together they gave him an air of self-assurance. It was precisely the look you would expect from the son of a lawyer and a doctor, and what's more, a doctor himself.

There had been no heating for some time. "Well, I don't know if I should've come with you," said Tomas.

I pointed at the empty seats: "Look, no one else is going There." A light gleamed in Tomas's eyes. The same light that linked us together and could endow everything with meaning; the light that kept us from taking God's name in vain as we set out together for There.

"But what kind of meaning?" I asked myself. "Some meaning in my departure and return?" Outside, my own country flashed past. But I was outside it. I was in transit to that other Country. Was I? I felt in my bones that the next few hours would transform me.

I went out into the corridor again. A little girl about two years old in a red coat was smiling at me from the nearest compartment door. When she saw that I was looking at her she grew serious, but I made a friendly grimace and once again she gave a little smile. She looked like a small goblin on a string. I hid behind the curtain, curious as to what she would do. She waited tensely. I stuck out my hand and made animal shapes for her. When I hid my hand she kept waiting. I stuck my hand out again and repeated the performance several times. When I grew weary of it I opened the window and leaned out. But outside there was a riverbed—that is, a future riverbed, in which stood bulldozers and excavators and great sheets of oilcloth stretched over sand. The icy air whipped my face and I gazed, as if in the grip of my own impotence, across the worksite to the old river. I gazed at the still enduring alder woods and the outflows of yellow sand on the banks, at the current that has been sweeping the sand away since the beginning of time, and at the hoar-frosted stalks of grass and the bush haunts of birds—at the entire riverbed of divine time that existed before man and might well have existed after him. But when I closed the window the little girl was still standing there. Since it looked as though I might pay attention to her again, she hopped happily up and down.

III

Metropolis. The Metropolis on our journey, dividing day from night. Metropolis, beyond which the rails we had to ride left the land and then returned to it once more, but this time in another world. First, however, we arrived at its station.

The dim hall echoed with the screeching of brakes and then everything fell silent. Even the fluorescent lighting went out and did not come back. Metropolis. I could walk out of the station and look into its life. I could take a walk on its soil. Or was it only an illusion? I sat in the mute compartment and the thoughts that had occurred to me that morning struck me once again. And yet I felt that I was already at the very threshold of metamorphosis—I could feel its mysterious breath. And I stepped out of the train . . . and like a sleepwalker I went out in front of the station and I looked down into illuminated streets where ribbons of cars stretched like veins of orange-black blood, and then like a sleepwalker I went back; the train started to move—at first slowly, very slowly, and then rapidly, like a machine set in unstoppable motion, and its direction was night.

On both sides houses flickered like timid witnesses to our story. I could hardly suppress my excitement. But the speed grew and the night was opening up. Inside reigned tension and immobility. The train lights went on again and the objects surrounding us took on a reddish glow as I fixed them with a gaze directed past their forms and into other spheres. Waiting in the deserted suburbs was "Otherwise." I shall always remember the somber space on which it stood, legs firmly planted, unspeaking. I leaned out the window and looked at small squares and into apartments whose interiors were still for a long time to break the surface, vanish, and finally escape. A sky full of stars took off at a run for the horizon like a speeded-up film, the wind rushed past and the rails rumbled; the sky ran up to the horizon and somewhere far ahead an invisible brush was coating it with a black paint that then dripped down onto the landscape—a winter landscape without snow. And I didn't want to look at it anymore; I fell back and at that moment our motion became fluid—the rails had already left the ground; night opened up and we plunged ever deeper into it. We lurched through the open night over bridges across precipices as open as the night, and we prayed with Hail Marys and Paternosters in words yet undiscovered—in the words with which everything begins and ends. And this was a sign that the transformation must begin. From my arm sprouted a tree; it broke through my sleeve and branched out over me luxuriantly: a mountain spruce with blue-green lichen on scented bark. My palm became strangely rigid and started to melt out and flow back. Yet it still remained mine (it was like a dream I had: someone is leaving, I want to wave at him and suddenly I can't tear my hand from the table surface). It changed into a ravaged rockface and into ice. At the same time one of my legs became a submachine gun, a bandage, and a flag, and the other—to my horror—started to change into a wolf's shank. Again I tried to enter into it in some way, but it was more organic than I. Before I could in any way grasp what was going on, an unknown force—as if by a trick—opened my heart and everything was flooded with my blood. Blood ran down the ice and the rockface and soaked into the bandage and the tree and I gazed on the scene as if in awe, but I felt no pain and only a peculiar estrangement—as if after a liter of red wine. The wine flowed and merged with the blood and from this mixture rose crowds of people whose faces engraved themselves in memory. The people then receded, carrying off in their bodies my belly, torso, and the remnants of my torn chest and I cried, "This is my blood which is spilt for you . . . and this is my body." This is what I screamed while losing my bearings in space and time because my head had lost its boundaries—I was groping for it with my only sound hand but what I grasped at were the labyrinths of villages and towns and the labyrinth of the whole earth with a multitude of shepherd's chalets in deserted mountains. And then the hand broke off and fell at the metamorphosed feet; but it immediately rose up and started dancing a wild dance that I understood only in part. It was the dance of metamorphoses and it took place on a plateau of broken rocks under a mountain spruce in the labyrinth of the dirty town. And the hand bowed . . . and became me. "Good," I said, "So from now on this is I. But what then?!" And the hand rose and became truth. "Good," I said, "But what then?!" And the hand pointed forward and became fate. I wanted to ask what next, but the hand rested on the spruce bark and was life. I had no need to ask further. But the hand clenched on the bark and was death.

And the hand danced on. It reeled on the wolf tracks bordering the frozen ground. It ran round the tree and staggered through city streets with the bandage tangled in clenched fingers. It sat down on a bench in a park. A man came and sat down beside it. The hand pointed and the man was put to flight. I pressed myself close to it. I laid my head in its palm. Its touch was both cooling and warming. "Be then myself and truth and fate and life and death," I told it.

IV

We reached the border of that Country ten minutes after midnight. On both sides of the tracks stood nineteen-year-old soldiers, submachine guns primed. Not a single one of them thought that he could be spending the night with his nearest and dearest. Not a single one of them envied us. We were carried on through, now at no more than a walking pace, past their dead eyes. The Country announced itself in the red color on the tracks and the green on coats. And in watchtowers and ramps with white light. The Country announced itself without divine omens.

Looking ahead—on tracks dissolving into misty air—it seemed unlikely that we would be able to slip through to the mountains. Those mountains, our desired destination. Out of the mist emerged a gelatinous shape that flowed out over the damp station ground. It was an oppressive feeling—ankle-deep everywhere—and it beat against the sides of our train as on the rocky shore of an ancient sea. A customs officer burst in from the corridor and howled, "Polaki!? Czeki!?" His unnecessarily violent movement dislodged the door from its runners.

"Czecki," we replied in kind. "Baggage!? Turisti!?" "Turisti." "Carabina, cocaine, hashish!?" "Nu." "Nu?" he responded in surprise, threw the door to the side, and vanished. Only an alcoholic haze remained behind him.

We tried to put the door back. The corridor rang with excited voices. An old grandma in country clothes was explaining something to the customs officer. On the floor lay an open suitcase and the officer's merciless hands were rifling through it. Several still unwrapped petticoats surfaced, some pullovers, and more and more clothes. The grandma was now simply standing there gaping down at her feet. Then she pulled a fistful of crumpled banknotes from her pocket and handed them to the customs officer. He tore them from her hand and tossed them on top of the rumpled clothes. He clicked the clasps shut and took the suitcase away with him.

The grandma followed him submissively. As she passed us she threw us an apologetic glance—as if to say: "Please don't think, young people, that we are a wicked nation."

We managed to close the door. A soldier stood listlessly under the window. I stuck my head out and he stretched a hand toward me, a demand that I give him a cigarette. With slight distaste at the way he took this demand for granted, I gave him one.

All around stood the motionless wagons of freight trains. Railway workers were running between the rails, striking the brakes with iron bars, and if I closed my eyes it seemed that the Country lying ahead was sending these sounds to meet us, and prepare us for the events of the days to come.

At last the train moved forward. "I'm going to the toilet," I said.

The toilet, still clean in Prague, was now unbelievably befouled. Behind the white tip-up windows passed a no-man's-land enclosed by barbed-wire.

I voided my sticky body with a feeling of disgust toward it. Then I set out back as quickly as possible. Where the corridor began I saw a gigantic man.

A kind of age-old quality emanated from him, and so the only thought to strike me was someone had conjured him here. His shaggy black coat indicated that he was a local and his black patent-leather shoes suggested a higher status. His confidence betrayed power. The corridor light was all that fell on his coarse face while the area in front of the toilet was dark. A face of license.

I tried to behave precisely as I would have done if I had seen nobody. But he barred my way with his arm and looked me straight in the eyes. I could manage nothing better than to point at myself and say, in an uncertain voice, "Czech"— as if to apologize for the fact that I was not the man he was after. "Cigareta!" he said, and I could smell the smoke on his breath. "Nu cigareta, nu fumati, nu fumati!" I explained. "Cigareta," he still shouted and grabbed me by the collar. I lost my footing. There was nobody to whom I could appeal for help. No words with which I could make myself understood. No blow with which to defend myself. I understood all this too well—the awareness led straight to passivity.

He dragged me to the passage between the cars and screamed something at me. Beneath us the wheels pounded on the rail joints. "Czech, Czech," I kept repeating in my confusion. By now it couldn't be simply a question of a cigarette. Of what then? And why?

But instead of stabbing me or throwing me from the train he left me alone. Suddenly he stood back facing me as if it had all been meant only as a warning. I walked away slowly. I still wanted to retain my dignity in my own eyes but in the corridor I was trembling like a leaf and had to lean against the wall. I looked back to see whether he was coming after me. No movement. Had he perhaps understood: "Nu cigareta"?

I stood in the middle of the corridor and didn't feel like going any further. I had always thought that in moments like this a man needs to look for a friend, but the reality was that I needed to find myself. At last I made up my mind to enter our compartment. Tomas raised his eyes and said, "What's up?" But immediately he added, "We have company."

Opposite Tomas sat a benignly smiling man with a beard—his air as natural as if he had always been there. He kept winking at me with bright eyes hidden deep in a thick growth of facial hair. The kind of eyes that offer you support. His coat was worn and shabby and layers of mud were peeling off his black boots. As he offered us smoked fat ham and bread his huge palms exuded suppleness.

I turned to Tomas and told him in roughly the following words, "Just outside the toilet an unknown man attacked me and wanted a cigarette off me. He dragged me into the passage between the carriages and tried to throttle me. In the end he let me go." I heard myself speak in the objective tones of a news report or a court testimony, and I terrified myself with the precision of my statement. As if Tomas and I needed some kind of proof, something we could hold on to, I automatically undid my shirt collar. Yes, they were there—the red imprints of fingers.

Just then the bearded man gave a meaningful grimace, bent down, and peeled a lump of clay from his boot. He opened the window slightly, threw the lump out and sat down. "That's the way it's done," those bright eyes sighed in relief.

And so time did not stand still and the noose did not tighten. We gasped for breath and life went on. The bearded man and Tomas were munching hunks of bread; the man shifted his hips and let out a prolonged fart.

The door opened. "This is the other one," said Tomas. "It's him," I said. In the doorway stood the man from the toilet. His glance slid across us without interest. I noticed that on the luggage rack—beside the bearded man's sack—lay a pigskin bag. The man in black was already one of us, then.

Silence fell. Only the bearded man kept munching his ham. I looked uneasily at the pack of cigarettes forgotten on the seat. When the unknown man noticed it, he was electrified. He reached into his overcoat and insistently pressed a blue bill on Tomas. Tomas froze and the strange man still more insistently pressed the bill into his hand. As if to say "You have to make this deal, you have to."

For us it was a very advantageous exchange. The cigarettes were one of the cheapest brands and if we had exchanged the bill for our money we could have bought more than twenty packs. This made the urgency with which the deal had been made even more puzzling.

The man in black took off his coat, exposing a light woolen pullover. His trousers were dark brown. His face evinced a gross, rather dull-witted triumph. I could not rid myself of the impression that this was not a natural role for him. At the same time I was sorry for him: he had traded on the level of African natives and was still proud of himself.

"Is there some town by the crossing point here?" asked Tomas. "I don't know of any," I answered thoughtfully. (I knew where the question was leading.) "And besides it doesn't seem likely," I continued, "that the local inhabitants would be allowed to board an express at the border crossing. But then again they don't have the luggage you'd expect for people traveling over the frontier. And I doubt that the bearded man is on an official journey."

"Then they simply ought not to be here on this train," repeated Tomas. "Then it's a mystery," he added.

I had to confess that I had no better ideas: maybe there was some town by the crossing and its inhabitants were allowed to get on express trains. These two were simply here, but backward their trail was lost, as if it had vanished. Or as if it were only in the train that it had started. Somewhere there, where we had left the borderline behind and plunged into no-man's-land—between the barbed-wire fences.

In the compartment the atmosphere became suffocating and Tomas began to grumble. (It was a no-smoking car.) I had to persuade him not to say anything. Irritated, he went out into the corridor.

I sat in the middle of the compartment, my back toward the journey's direction. On my left sat the man with the beard. The other man sat opposite me. They were beginning to interest me.

When Tomas had gone out, the bearded man asked me genially: "Problem?" (Apparently he had the knack of perceiving everything.) "Nu . . . nu problem." I stuttered.

I was now able to see them and compare them better. In fact they were not so dissimilar as they had seemed at first. They could have both been about forty and both were robust with prominent cheekbones.

Tomas came back. The bearded man pulled down his sack and dug out a bottle of spirits. He handed it to Tomas, who said "Tomas," and drank.

Then I was given the bottle. I said "Martin," and did the same.

The bottle went back to the man with the beard. He pointed at himself as if to show both what he was and what he was fated to be. As if to say: "I will never be anything else." And he said: "Remu." "Remu," we couldn't help repeating the name.

Remu handed the bottle to the man at the door. He slowly raised it to his lips. He tilted back his head and poured a vast proportion of the bottle's transparent contents down his throat. "Romu," he burst out proudly. Beyond the window glittered the lights of the first large town.

v

The corridor slowly started to fill up. The train kept stopping and at every station the number of people standing there increased. But nobody came into our compartment. Through the crack in the door seeped a strong sweetish smell. It was a smell that these people brought on their coats, shoes, and clothes, and it somehow enveloped them without their having in any way caused it. It must have originated deep in the womb of that Country. In the womb of the homes of these simple people and in the womb of their large clean wardrobes made of clean beechwood.

Romu and Remu were both without it. There was no smell emanating from their possessions. Here in this environment it was astonishing. Once again I felt the obscurity of their past. Time passed slowly. Tomas slept by the window. The other two as well, each in his own way, were immersed in themselves. Romu was relishing his power and strength. Remu, for his part, was savoring his capacity to take life as it was. As the kilometers went by I noticed that despite their apparent indifference to each other there was some relationship between them. They were aware of each other. I sensed how the smallest of Remu's expressions sent Romu berserk. How he was provoked by Remu's frivolity, which he so lacked. Romu was certainly very tall. He had strong cheekbones and strong jaws. It wouldn't be easy to break them with a blow of the fist. But Remu was no lightweight either. He accepted Romu's resentment with unending tolerance.

Now he stood up and went out. When he returned he exchanged a few words with Romu. Romu too uttered several incomprehensible sentences. I was suddenly assailed by suspicion: What if these two were in cahoots? What if this was a trap? . . . Under the surface something was happening and there was nothing to catch hold of. Perversely, I felt an urge to go to the toilet. I knew that sooner or later I would have to go. I prodded the sleeping Tomas with my hand."I need to go to the toilet and after my last experience I don't want to go alone." (Tomas was peering at me with sleepy eyes.) "A moment ago these two were discussing something. I'm afraid they may be in cahoots."

"Do you think they want to rob us?" Tomas yawned drowsily, but realistically. "I don't know," I shrugged my shoulders.

"But if we both go, it will be more likely," he said. I had to admit he had a point. "Never mind," I said. "It was just a strange feeling." And I resolved to go to the toilet by myself.

"I have to go as well, anyway," volunteered Tomas.

"So are we going?"

And so we went out.

We pushed through the corridor between the local people. On the floor were heaped suitcases, sacks, and even some crates. And everywhere that sweetish smell. "Where are they all going, for God's sake?" wondered Tomas. "There are only a few connections here," I proffered my guess as if I had been certain.

In front of the toilet stood a slight dark-haired girl. While I waited for Tomas she fixed me with her deep eyes. They were the enchanter's eyes of a child prematurely awakened into womanhood. They were eyes swimming like two bottomless wells of passion. Within a couple of years life would exact the price of this early conflagration with sudden decay. But now she was still something that gripped a man's heart like a mixture of ice and scorching coal.

Where had all these people come from and where were they going, for God's sake? Where, at just this moment, were they dragging the destinies linked to this Country? I had to admit I didn't know. Something was announcing itself through them—something I could only glimpse. It attracted and at the same time repelled me.

We returned. Romu pulled out the cigarettes that he had bought at so high a price. He lit one and smoked it rapidly and without enjoyment. When it was nearly finished he lit a second from the stub. And then a third. At the corner by the window Remu snored noisily. He made a charming picture—a shapeless black beard flowing around his head. I ceased to be afraid.

Suddenly I couldn't believe that we would get off the train and these two would vanish. I was quite unable to imagine us alighting. Inside there was still some security. At least we didn't have to think about what would happen next.

The tension between the inside and the outside grew. So too the tension between the present and the future. There remained only the last few hours of the journey. Beyond the window lay the darkness and in the darkness that other Country. Yes, it was there. I could clearly sense its contours: its vast body covered with the still impenetrable garment of night. Its streams flowing freely in meadows. The pastures reaching to the thresholds of houses.

I was slowly sinking into sleep. I dreamed that Romu and Remu were standing over me. Then I dreamed that they were taking their leave of us. "Happy Christmas," they were saying in Czech.

THE TOWN ENCOUNTERED AT SUNRISE

I

A SEVERE VOICE, URGING SOME ACTION, SOUNDED FROM THE loudspeakers. The words reverberated and fell into the crowd of people like bales of burning straw. Something unusual was going on. I saw local faces inflamed with anger and impotence. A local family, stumbling over cases and bundles, was pushing toward the exit.

At last we reached the steps leading to the train and tried to press upward against the current of people. The international screech of a gypsy woman sliced through the space beside us. "Do you think that any trains will be running?" Tomas shouted at me from a step above. "It doesn't look like it."

We stepped up onto the platform; nothing now gaped at us from its white cement blocks but a brightly colored scarf, lying there in token of departure. Far away in front a double-decker train stood mute, and at a distance of about fifty meters a line of soldiers stretched right across the platform. Hesitantly we stepped into the empty space and realized that this branch-line train, which was to have taken us to the starting point of our journey, would not be setting off. We realized that not a single train would be leaving the station—somehow it was written all over the soldiers and the people and we didn't have to go any further to confirm it, but we walked on. (There was nowhere to retreat.)

We slowly drew closer to the soldiers. The loudspeakers fell silent and the station lay prostrate before us in choked rigidity. The rays of a December sunrise slipped over the roof of the waiting room. A few of them reached the pavement and myopically flickered between the soldiers and ourselves. The cold was shattering.

As we neared the center of the empty space I started toying with the idea that there would be an explosion of gunfire. Somewhere inside me thundered, "Take aim," and on all sides cold machine-gun barrels were rising. I smelled vaseline. "Fire!"

The station was quite small and fairly modern. The platform on which we stood actually consisted of a large area adjoining a one-story hall that had once been designed as a pleasant pavilion for a moment's rest.

"Isn't it dangerous?" said Tomas in a strangled voice.

"Most probably yes," I nodded, and I was glad that once again he had been the first to say it. Our steps became distinctly shorter. "We'll go right up to them," I continued, "And then we'll see." But Tomas had his own opinion because he stopped and pretended to tie his shoelace. "Don't be crazy," I hissed at him under my breath, "We can't stop here!" He didn't listen—he took off his rucksack and knelt down to unfasten a strap. "Are you listening?" I tried to plead with him. "We'll go on and we'll pretend we don't have any idea something's wrong."

Pretend we don't have any idea something's wrong. But how? Silence closed over us and became a maelstrom. (It was not silence but refusal to break silence.) I slipped the straps off my shoulders.

Then there was a crackling and from the loudspeakers came the same incomprehensible voice. It didn't say "Hands up!" or "Give yourselves up!" Perhaps it wasn't even addressing us, but we felt the dark night and the shining beam of the reflectors flattening us against the cement plain. It was a plain spread over the boundaries of the heavenly spheres and a man walking across it was outcast, like an ant on a Formica tabletop. Its edges fall sheer into eternal fixity, into space without life or form.

At that moment I noticed a small group of people. Yes, people. To all appearances it was a family: father, mother, grown-up son and slightly younger daughter—the jewel of the family. They were standing in a recess of the station hall and I saw that they were debating something. I had the impression that the something was us.

We made a rampart of our rucksacks and looked around us. At first anxiously and then with curiosity. The voice from the loudspeakers was now more relaxed and sounded kindlier. At a distance of twenty meters even the soldiers were only people. Their ranks were uneven and they were not deathly serious.

Why can there be no shortcut on the path of destiny? Why didn't it occur to us, as any of these moments passed, to turn back? We had a single goal and we were unable to give it up, although we knew that it was impossible. An unknown force was pushing us to the very edge of that impossibility.

Once again my eyes wandered toward the foursome. Some old-world air of cultivation, which purified them, made them stand out from their surroundings. They were wearing long, pale, fur coats and their large number of suitcases gave the impression that they were on their way to some mountain sanatorium, a resort visited fifty years ago. It was so convincing a picture that a wave of grief shot through me for all the mountain sanatoriums of this Country, destroyed by communism and by time. Now they were picking up their cases and with dignity—as if by their own decision and not for fear—were walking to the steps. The father separated himself from them and came toward us at a rapid pace.

"You can't stand here," he said in German. "They will not permit it." And I knew what he was saying even if I understood practically nothing. I contemplated his half-wrinkled face, which looked as if rid of cares by the continuous exhaustion of a life under threat. It was a face from which anxiety, bitterness, and fear had been forced to depart, which even the bitter cold had not deprived of its deeply engrained pallor.

"Don't stay here! There's a State of Emergency." His family had stopped at the top of the steps and was waiting. He realized that he had to return to them. Halfway back, however, he turned around and once again urged us to leave. We went.

"You said it would be safe here," said Tomas reproachfully as we neared the steps. It was true. This Country as I had known it was not dangerous, but strange. Only at times had the hopelessness surfaced on the suffering faces of the majority of its people, and only at times had the insensitive attitudes of its authorities aroused tension. The grandmother apologizing for her misconduct in the corridor of the international train: that was the Country as I had known it. But a State of Emergency?

We slowly descended the steps, as if coming down from mountain plains to earthly reality. At the edge of this reality stood two village mothers with their infants bound to their bodies. They were standing at the boundary between the corridor and the steps like worn figurines from war films. But in fact like light and shadow, like night and day. Their story was simple: they had gone on a visit to the town because it was a holiday, they had relied on something that had always worked, but the world had gone off the rails. We went around them and tried not to meet their eyes.

"Isn't it great," said Tomas, "Just imagine your future wife going out with the baby and it ending this way." He didn't have to say it. Now I had to add some generalization to silence my conscience. "This is what happens," I said, "when we're betrayed by things that we don't even know we surrounded ourselves with." But in fact, in uttering this generalization I wounded myself even more: What in God's name would these two women do? The question resounded in my head. Where would they go on this freezing December day? Who would feed their children? And you, God, what do you say to this? What journey back will you prepare for them?

The number of people in the corridor increased and we tried not to lose the family from the platform. It was our only handhold. But I reflected, at the sight of the charming daughter's long light-brown braid, the mother's tall figure heightened by the fur hat, the brother's broad shoulders and the tired rigidity of the father, that it was precisely these people who might have taken the two women home with them. I would have expected them to do it. Yet we entered the large hall and I grasped that it was senseless to ask such a thing of them. All around reigned indescribable chaos, noise, and stench. People were literally squeezed together everywhere; baggage, children, old people. . . . A drunken old man at our feet mumbled something and stank of urine. A staleness had set into the faces. There was no color in sight. Everything was equally wretched—gray or black, streaked or white; a place of dry bread, with at best a little speck or homebrew. The suffering of an individual was no more than a drop in the oceanic ignorance of authorities who had visibly abandoned all obligations toward the people of the Country. Indeed, it would be senseless to ask anything of anyone. "This is genocide," I told Tomas, who was gazing around us in fright.

"Or simply civil war," ventured Tomas, exaggerating.

But the mood was low. Oppressed, afraid. As if only recently something terrible had happened, something still fresh in the memory. The platforms were empty. The steps and corridors were also quiet. There was no protest, from anyone, anywhere. The crowd behaved like a frightened animal cowering in the furthest corner of the cage.

In the face of this mass helplessness our own situation, too, became burdensome. I had actually got what I wanted. I had left Prague—its solid safety. The modern world had started to seem to me like an artificially arranged shopwindow, and the lives within it like a professionally scripted television film. Individual originality had been forced into the mold of a standardized humankind. Nothing remained but to copy out the copy and compare it with the example prescribed within the framework of generally applicable prosperity. No "worry" or even "worrying." "Getting oneself that little bit extra" was the state of the everyday modern world. We, however, were standing in the station concourse of that Country under a State of Emergency. It was a reality almost too real. "Reality is for the local people, " said my skeptical "I." "For you this is at most some attraction you've been drawn into. Tourist!"

I was especially touchy about the word "tourist." Why tourist? Why not "pilgrim," for example? I objected heatedly. "This is my sacred pilgrimage. And the danger threatening these people is real for me as well, because every danger that threatens people anywhere in the world also menaces me. The State of Emergency that has been declared here, showing the ruling group's complete loss of touch with the interests of the citizens, immediately threatens my own corrupted country. There too the rights of the individual are no more than grains of sand under the feet of the powerful. My father and my mother are threatened by this state of affairs, and so too is my future wife when she sets out with our future child for the neighboring town. The danger is also mine."

"Good," said my skeptical "I," "but you had some inkling of how it might be here. And you knew you would hardly change anything here. So why did you come? You exposed yourself to danger artificially, and that's not an experience. It's an intellectual experiment."

"Perhaps it's fate," I countered.

"And there's no train back," I said, once again.

A new wave of loudspeaker announcements now descended on our heads. We were already at the exit from the station hall, and we turned and saw, over the heads of those surrounding us, the edge of the upper terrace, likewise crammed with people waiting for a connection. In the sticky atmosphere I felt small drops of perspiration emerging under my layers of clothing.

We walked out and a gust of icy wind opened and cleaned us. Anyone expecting a town would have been disappointed. Nothing but wide unused flat spaces with blocks of concrete housing scattered haphazardly and stretching far into the distance. Only at the very edges of these spaces rose heaps of rubble with pieces of wall here and there and only behind them an uninterrupted built-up town area, the closest houses bearing the unmistakable marks of mass demolition. "They have stolen the heart of the town," it occurred to me as I pictured the time when even here and by the station there had been streets, lanes, and little squares—the veins and arteries through which the town's blood circulated. The concrete housing blocks were five storys high and their walls almost black, as if smoked by sooty smog. Behind them—directly facing us—the bloodless disk of the sun stood on the horizon. To the south rose the forested hilltops and white wads of cloud were nearing the edges of the houses. A thin dirty covering of iced-over snow was clinging to the ground.

"There's nothing for it," said Tomas. "If we can't find a place to sleep we'll go to the mountains beyond the town."

"And if we don't have much food, then we'll eat less," I said. In fact we had quite enough food and the idea that we might have to sleep outside the town was one that I didn't take seriously. If something was happening I wanted to be there. I knew my attitude flew in the face of all the parental rules that inevitably accompanied me on my journeys even though I was grown-up. Because it would be sensible to stay in the train station and go back at the first opportunity. But from childhood I had cultivated in myself an unfulfilled longing to fight against dictatorship. I wanted to use my own strength to strike at it at least once in my lifetime. News of uprisings that had broken out in distant parts of the world excited me. And the idea that I would be able to experience such an event . . . ?

The four were moving away along one of the well-trodden paths. We passed a decayed bus park and slowly caught up with them. The father and brother were walking on the outside and keeping both women under their protection. They were stumbling a little on the icy path and stood out as a foursome; it even seemed that a dark glow surrounded them (even though more careful scrutiny found none). Perhaps it was the vocation that they carried simply by being themselves. But the nature of this vocation I did not know.

Romu and Remu had stood out in the same way. Yes, those two. But they had been lost to us as we left the train. I looked around to see if I could catch a glimpse of them somewhere in the empty space speckled with individuals and small groups of people. But they were not there. Nevertheless something told me that I would meet them again. In the distance I saw some children. "Do you think," I said hesitantly, "that if we lived here we still wouldn't have taken those two women home with us?"

"Would you saddle yourself with two mothers and children at a time like this?" Tomas responded in disbelief, "You've no idea how long it could last. And how would you feed them!? No, Martin, it's terribly difficult. And in the end a husband would turn up from some village and knife you."

What he said was true. I probably wouldn't have taken them home either. But it upset me (perhaps just for this reason) that he kept insisting on such a superficial view. "You're a typical doctor," I thought reproachfully. "For years they've taught you that you needn't and mustn't take human destinies on your shoulders."

We slowed down so as not to catch up with the family ahead of us. The sun swung a little higher, but the wads of cloud were also shifting. On the right was a blackened concrete house; its windows were incomprehensibly small and hung with laundry from the inside. We tried to maintain a distance of twenty meters.

The foursome reached the corner of the house and stopped there. We stopped as well and pretended to be looking around. In fact we were looking nowhere and our throats were constricted with anxiety.

"You're expecting them to take you with them," my skeptical "I" spoke into the silence. This time I didn't contradict it. What other way should we take when theirs was the true one?

At last the father once again separated himself from the group and retraced his steps toward us. The decision had been taken.

There was no time for smiles of greeting; no time for the kindness of the charming daughter or the brother's assurances that he would stand by us. We swiftly joined their group. It was exactly as we had expected.

The darkening clouds gathered themselves into the shape of a great bird whose wings covered the sun. It extinguished the shimmer of morning, and fresh, sharp gusts blew from the town. It was one of those moments when the image of a tiled bathroom with hot water was more vivid than ever.

Beside the path a cloth billboard slogan was lying on the snow. Most probably it bore the legend, "For better tomorrows."

A five-pointed red star edged out of a nearby burrow. "That's where I was," it pointed grimly to a pole not far away, "And now I'm left to . . . ugh!" It spat out a huge wad of phlegm. As I observed its scowl I wanted to throw a frozen clod at it, but menace still emanated from its smart-aleck mouth. "But just you wait . . ." and it gushed out a bucketful of dirty water. Then it dried its wet points on its apron. "This fucking, freezing weather," it grimaced. "And at Christmas too," it added. "And that stinking gypsy comes to shit in front of my burrow. The bitch," it addressed the empty air but it was still clear that the remark was directed at someone who wasn't supposed to miss it.

A wizened gypsy appeared at the opening of a neighboring burrow. "Shut your mouth, you old proletarian hag," she yelled in gypsy. "A bit of gypsy shit won't hurt you. You cunt!"

"Yours stinks at five meters, you fucked-up twat." The star could not be shouted down. (Apparently it had got used to its new conditions.) "And you wipe your ass with your underwear, so fuck off back to your shit-hole!" And the star advanced threateningly.

"So you don't like the smell of my gypsy ass?" screamed the gypsy. "It doesn't like the smell of my gypsy ass," and she squatted so shamelessly that her asshole gleamed above the gray snow. "It would even steal the ass off a gypsy, the red cunt," she yelled at the cloudy sky.

"Look! Soldiers," I whispered in a strained voice. On the other side of the wide empty road stood a military patrol. And a little further away another. And on the opposite side yet another one. "And look, there's an overturned bus." I pointed diagonally forward. The bus lay at the edge of a completely straight road. In fact it was only a wreck—when they overturned it, it must already have been very old. In this Country there was no other kind.

The brother noticed our excitement and nodded in agreement. As if to say, "That's the way it looks here."

We turned to the right. "Will it take long?" asked Tomas in German. This time the sister turned to him. "We live one kilometer from here," she said. Her face lit up with the need to establish friendly relations. I envied Tomas the fact that he had been the first to speak with her.

To left and right heaps of rubble mounted and the old apartment houses that apparently made up the core of the town came closer. Clearance. But the progressive slogans, hammered into the frozen ground on the edges of the demolition site, were overgrown with thick bushes. In the embankments several burrows yawned darkly and the snow in front of them was trodden down. To all appearances the demolition site was alive.

At last we slipped into streets that were almost empty. A dry icy wind scorched everything. On both sides we could glimpse shopwindows. But today the shops were closed. In distant and at this moment almost forgotten Prague it used to be the custom to decorate the Christmas shopwindows with silver chains and glass balls. Here too there was one big blue ball and two chains over an orderly line of dry biscuits.

In distant and almost unreal Prague. Already thousands of people had set out on their holiday stroll. Amply fed, some of them even stuffed; there was still enough food and warmth for everyone. Nevertheless I felt that something important was lacking there. And lacking too some hundreds of kilometers further on, where the pulse of Paris and London was beating to a holiday rhythm. The whole civilized world. In the last month the biggest hit with the advertising agencies had been close-ups of children's eyes.

Only now and then did someone pass us on the sidewalk. The sidewalk was as untended as everything here and the foursome began to strike me as very lonely. More and more frequently I leaned sideways to see their faces, at least for a moment. Now they had one main worry: not to fall on the icy surface. The father was supporting the stumbling mother, who was too tall. At times suppressed sighs slipped from her lips. The daughter walked on the left. Her thin face with its narrow mouth and high forehead, at first sight unremarkable, drew my eyes. Now she also looked at me. I would have guessed her age at twenty-three.

At the end of the street there was a humming of motors. A column of military vehicles was approaching from the town center. "Into the house!" the father pointed. We piled through a half-open front door. Immediately the rumbling silhouettes of vehicles started to flash through the street. Behind the massive door lay safety and calm. Suddenly we were all standing together. "You never know," the father said apologetically in German and put an arm around his wife's shoulders. "This is my wife Mirela, my son Andrei, and my daughter Livie. And I am Simeonu. Simeonu Cudean."

"I am Martin and this is Tomas. From Prague." (German became our language of communication.)

"Prague," smiled Mme. Mirela and her eyes glittered as if with an unfulfilled dream.

"You should understand that my wife was once in Prague when she was young," said the father. "But you probably wanted to go to the mountains. It will be difficult for you to get there now," he shrugged helplessly.

"This is much more interesting for us," I said. "Of course: the mountains are always the same, but a State of Emergency?" seconded Tomas.

They smiled. Livie smiled as she stood at Andrei's side. She didn't know that a strip of light was falling through the gap between door and frame onto her face, dividing it into two equally welcoming parts. "Mother loves her memories of Prague, " she said. We walked back through the door into the cold December day.

II

We were negotiating the steep, zigzag staircase with great difficulty. Seen from inside, the house bore almost too great a resemblance to any house in Prague. Simply worked banisters, rows of large doors, shadowy recesses. We climbed ever higher: one story, two storys. I was terribly stiff from sitting—from the wakeful night, from the train, from the long wait. And this private apartment above the stairs on the fourth and last story: would it be more than simply another paralyzing waiting room . . . awaiting change? Return?

We reached its door. This was smaller than the others and white. The father Simeonu turned the key and light from the corridor fell onto the black-and-white marble floor of the entrance hall. "But we can't intrude on them like this, " I thought suddenly. And immediately I said so. They too were seized by embarrassment and, in their very eagerness to please, forgot what they were supposed to be doing. I picked up the suitcase which Mme. Mirela had put down and dragged it over the wooden threshold onto the floor. But I couldn't rid myself of the sense that this floor was terribly familiar to them and terribly strange to us . . . and that with our presence it would become strange to them as well. I felt that their home would lose its former face for them. I looked at Tomas, waiting for his reaction, but he just shrugged even though he too would certainly have welcomed some liberating solution. "And is there any other place we can go?" he asked.

Simeonu noticed our hesitation and nodded: "Come in; come in."

"I'm afraid," I began with embarrassment, "that we ought not to impose on you. It's a holiday and I'm sure you just want to be with your family."

"At the moment every one of us in danger counts as family," he countered good-naturedly, and two puckish sparks of laughter flashed in his eyes—just as they had in Remu's. It was as if he had said: "All these authorities can kiss our asses."

The door closed behind us. "After all, there's nothing at stake yet," said Tomas in Czech, "we can stay here for two hours and then leave. Or just stay until evening. We'll see if it bothers them. But Martin, these people have a completely different way of thinking. Even if they wanted to throw us out, they would be most offended by our refusing their hospitality."

We stood in the hall, suddenly pressed against each other. Livie and her mother disappeared. Three other doors gave no hint of what was hidden behind them. But the two women had most probably gone to tidy up. Simeonu moved quickly toward us and put first my rucksack and then Tomas's down on the floor. His soft cultivated hands made a striking contrast to the torn canvas and at the same time suited it. It was the same with the world in which he lived. Only a weak striplight shone in the hall. Under it was a zinc basin without a tap. Andrei stood leaning against it and smiling neutrally. He was probably wondering what had got into his father.

Simeonu certainly looked transformed. He fussed around us and beamed. "Put your jackets here—as you like—just as you like. But it's cold in the apartment—unfortunately." As if we were bringing some liberating and long-awaited break. A break in the inescapable series of days. "And this is our main room."

It was large with a high ceiling and an old carpet on long strips of unpolished parquet. On the left was the entrance to the kitchen. The wall curved into an alcove at each of two windows. I cast a surreptitious glance down into the street. Extraordinarily little from the outside world penetrated into the apartment. The objects here were immobilized—almost foreign, old, but not antique or especially ostentatious. One of them, emerging into the unremarkable foreground, was a Jewish Hanukkah candlestick standing on a bookshelf. "So that's how it is, then," I thought when I saw it. By the door to the kitchen a radio of local manufacture gave a tinny grin.

Livie came out of the kitchen and brought tea. "To warm us up," she said and put the tray on the wooden table. "Good idea," said the father and gently touched his daughter's hands. "I won't drink yet—I have to unpack and think things over—sit down and drink. And now excuse me—for a moment."

We settled ourselves in upholstered armchairs. I turned to Livie: "What do you feel about being home again?" She shrugged a little sadly. "We're used to it," she said in an altered voice; she smiled and tears welled up in her eyes. I envied her pure German. But I would probably have understood her even if she had spoken in an entirely incomprehensible language.

We were silent and could feel that she liked being with us even though we weren't speaking. For no other reason than her uncertainty whether we liked it too, she finally got up and went out. "Thanks for the tea," Tomas was faster than I.

We were left by ourselves in the room. Sunk in the old armchairs we sipped hot tea. "They could have taken in somebody quite different," it occurred to me. Those two mothers, for example—who had needed it so much. Perhaps too much. They would have been a burden while we were still an excitement. And so they had taken us. It was the same old injury inflicted again and again on the truly poor—those unable even to be interesting to somebody.

But we could have said: "Don't take us—take them—their need is greater."

There it was. I stood up and pulled aside the curtain from the nearer of the windows. On the other side and over the housetops I saw forested hills falling steeply. In clearings the patchy snow glistened. The unkindness of the station was forgotten and it seemed to me that I was suffocating. I was hidden here unnecessarily when I should have been climbing toward the ridges through the icy air. We could perhaps have gone. Perhaps a car might have stopped for us. I looked down. But the road was empty. Tomas appeared beside me. "From the fourth floor the State of Emergency isn't so interesting," he said, because he had a habit of throwing back the thoughts he guessed at. But I had been serious.

"You'll get scared of what's outside, and the mountains, before you're even out of the house," my skeptical "I" declared confidently. But I got the better of it by honesty: "I'm already scared now," I said. It was a war of nerves. Nothing in me wanted to leave. I felt fine; I was even curious to find out how such a local family lived. But something still drove me away. And it was not some external reason—it was inside me. Only I myself wanted to stay and I was the only thing driving myself away. And I drove myself away.

"Shall we go?" I asked after a while.

"You want to leave?" He paused. "And what if nothing is running?"

"We can try and hitch a lift."

"And if there aren't any cars?"

"We'll go to the mountains behind the town."

He considered. "Well, I don't know," he said. "The truth is that it's silly to take a rest immediately after you've arrived: do we really deserve a rest yet?" As I was listening to him I was yet again uncertain whether these thoughts were mine or his. When I was with him I never knew which was him and which was me.

"So shall we leave immediately?" he asked.

"Immediately," I said and inwardly cursed myself for it. I turned away from the window. In front of me stretched the room and the fact that I had pushed us into something that I didn't want. The radio was grimacing and the candlestick stood mute. I hoped that something would happen to force us to stay without our having to reproach ourselves. Maybe a bomb would go off in the street or shooting would start. "Are you going to tell them?" ventured Tomas. "Why just me, we'll both tell them." "And what are we going to tell them?" "We'll say that we're trying to get to the mountains. And that if we don't make it we'll come back." As I said this, I noticed the rows of books. Arranged in short lines on the desk, the shelves, and in the bookcase, they blocked my path. I tried to read one spine but it meant nothing to me.

THE TOWN ENCOUNTERED AT SUNRISE

Cold emanated from the ground and the walls. The central heating wasn't working and the stove was unlit. The weight of parting descended on me. I saw Livie—incomprehensibly illuminated and yet ordinary—with nearsighted blue eyes under a high forehead: her thin figure tenderly wrapped in the folds of her dress. Mme. Mirela: she was undoubtedly looking forward to our stories about Prague. Andrei . . . it was hard to say what he thought. But the father was sincerely pleased. And I . . . it was as if I was betraying them by our departure.

"So are we really going?" I turned to Tomas.

"Or maybe not?" he said.

We went back to the window and looked at each other indecisively. "It'll be cold there." "But beautiful."

When we entered the hall there was no one there and the bulb over the sink was dead. But from the furthest half-opened door voices could be heard. "It's a pity," I said, "that we didn't meet them at the end of the trip. I'd like to spend a few days with them."

In the room Simeonu and Mirela were standing over a marital bed overflowing with unpacked things. The empty suitcases had been discarded by the door.

"We came to tell you," I started with embarassment, "we've decided to try to get to the mountains."

"But it's impossible," exclaimed Simeonu in surprise, and Mirela, the only one who didn't understand German, gave him a questioning look. "Look, we wanted to go to the mountains as well," he pointed at their unpacked belongings. Then he turned to his wife and it was clear what he was saying. They had both already changed into their house clothes and I was surprised at how old they were. A thick sweater had absorbed all the tension from the father's face. His mouth had slackened, his brow had wrinkled, and only his wisdom, harnessed to the everyday struggle to survive, remained. Thick patched track pants made his body shorter.

Mirela wore the same and her bottom protruded strangely over long thin legs.

"We know," I started again, "that it is probably unwise. But we have to try it for our own peace of mind. After all, that's why we came. Don't be offended that we've caused you bother. And if it's all right with you, it's possible that we may still come back today. Or some other day. If you don't mind."

Simeonu looked sad. It was clear he was disappointed but he understood. He rose from his unpacking and came with us to the hall. "Wouldn't you like to wait at least until the afternoon?" Livie came too, but it was already too late to withdraw. "We'll leave right away."

We started to adjust our luggage and they stood over us. "I'll give Livie the chocolate," I said in Czech.

"And I'll give her Christmas cookies," said Tomas.

"Why give her Christmas cookies. It's enough that I'm giving her chocolate," I said in annoyance.

"It's not enough," he said with a self-assured air, "I want to give her something too."

"It was my idea," I hissed, "give Mirela some coffee instead."

"Why? I'll give her a tin of meat." And Tomas fished a tin and Christmas cookies out of his rucksack.

"Are you serious?" I said sadly.

"I am," he said cheerfully.

I approached Livie second. What did it matter? I wasn't the only one and I couldn't have this moment to myself. "So maybe we won't see each other again," I said. "But if someday you could come and see Prague, if you wanted, I would invite you."

"Really?" she exclaimed and was suddenly transformed. "I would love that," and she ran to get a pencil. I watched her delight as if from a distance, and I could scarcely believe that I had caused it. It probably wasn't difficult to make her happy. She and sadness had little in common, even in this

THE TOWN ENCOUNTERED AT SUNRISE

time of upheaval. She was a creature of sun, flowers, and warm breezes and she needed all these to be able to live. But on every side there was cold. And gloom. And darkness. And yet she lived. Her hair wasn't fair. It was only peculiarly fine.

We opened the door to the corridor and an icy gust hit us from below. "The only possibility," said Simeonu, "is to walk to the first village and then ask someone there to arrange a horsecart. No one has gas these days. And it would be very dangerous. This street will take you to the north edge of the town. It used to be called the North-South Road."

"And so we'll take a walk through the town and we'll be back soon," said Tomas with a smile.

"Bon voyage," said Andrei.

The door slammed. We walked down the stairs and I had the feeling I had nothing more to say to Tomas. So much malice. So much wasted effort to wrong-foot me.

"Shall we do what he said?" he asked.

"It doesn't matter."

He would just keep asking. As if posing questions were more important than what he thought himself. And what did he really think?

"You think it's wrong that I gave Livie the Christmas cookies?"

"Give me a break!"

The cold increased. It was like at the beginning: senseless. No faith, only steps leading forward out of necessity. I recalled Prague. We had walked out into the street and it had already been decided how everything would be. The north wind was carrying the sharp mountain air into the town.

"Do you think that she'll come one day?" asked Tomas placatingly. But my eyes and my thoughts at that moment were aimed (as if bewitched by the unsolvable code of what they perceived) under Tomas's chin, back in the direction we had come from. Who was the man in the black coat standing by the gray-pink house perhaps a hundred and fifty meters away? It was too far for me to be sure but too close for doubts. It was Romu.

I jerked my head toward him.

"You mean the one in black?"

"Him."

Tomas too was visibly disturbed and would rather not look. There was no doubt that the man in the black coat, whoever he was, was there because of us. At least that's how we saw it. But why?

We crossed over to the opposite sidewalk and set off along the former North-South Road to the north. Away from the station. The unknown man who had been standing on the south side stayed behind us. Nevertheless I felt his unmoving presence.

My eyes wandered to the fourth floor, but there were several different convex windows. And what if the man in black was there because of them? I started to be afraid for myself and for them.

The street in front of us curved and widened. To the left a small town park appeared. A pair of lovers frolicked between the benches and this calmed us down. But the park itself was unkempt. Pissed on, spat on, trampled. "What's there left to say?" shouted the nearest bench. "This is a place of dust and ashes." And it was.

I realized that we were leaving the people who a moment before had been entertaining us in this unholy mess. And if anything happened to them we would probably never know.

Another pair walked past us. They looked foolish. He had a high sheepskin hat and he wore his hair idiotically cut round his ears. She was mindlessly holding his arm.

We reached a large crossroads where a military escort reminded the passers-by of the State of Emergency. A bent old woman was selling chesspieces of various sizes here. I had never stopped feeling that someone was following me, but here—with the increase in passers-by—the feeling dispersed (not that it vanished entirely). We hesitated over which way to go. To go north on the North-South Road was somehow too easy. It stretched away irrevocably while the real core of the town seemed to begin to the left.

We set out toward the town's core and after a moment everything lit up and broadened out. Above us was an ostentatious administrative building (once a summer residence or chateau) with shattered windowpanes. Marble symbols of power and fragments of progressive mosaics were strewn on the sidewalk. Sleepy glaziers with frost-reddened hands were working on the lowest windows. One of them apathetically leaned toward us and bawled out: "Cigareta?"

"The local incantation," I thought, rummaging through my pockets.

Even today quite a number of people had come out for a kind of traditional stroll. But acquaintances stopped to greet each other only for a moment and rapidly took their leave. It looked like the last outing before some looming event. The torn-up paving-stones and shredded posters pointed to recent days. Here and there soldiers' submachine guns recalled the present. And the mood was ripening for tomorrow. Sometimes it manifested itself in the short hesitation of someone who had perhaps seen the paving-stone he had thrown yesterday, and in his evasive glance—seemingly wary of itself and then returning full of defiance. And on top of this was my obsessive idea that I could glimpse a black coat. I saw it everywhere I least expected it.

Only further on, in the valley between two high hills, lay the center of the town. The demolition, maybe frightened of the anger of the unusually silent mountains, did not yet threaten to reach this far. The sky clouded over and I felt that it would get warmer. A colony of ravens had settled in the trees by a small chapel. The wooden superstructures on the two- or three-story houses shared the pitch-black color of their bodies. A half-fallen world of galleries, balconies, and staircases. But some houses looked as if recently repaired. The street we had just been walking down had even turned into a kind of representative town thoroughfare, fronted with more or less well-arranged shopwindows and running toward a square.

Here—by a small church—it was absolutely quiet. We approached the iron door over the crunching remnants of snow. The door was ajar. Inside, a cavernous darkness reigned and innumerable candles flickered. Those who had crept in here like overcoated shadows were lighting others with trembling hands, investing them with their joyless faith.

"This is not joylessness," said the iron door, reading my thoughts. "It only looks that way to you because you are not living righteously."

"I see nothing of God here," I said. "Where is the light of his wisdom and love? Where is the warming brightness?"

What I saw were only the failing flames of human destinies. Terrified, uncertainly flickering through the darkness; scarcely distancing themselves from the stone floor by a few inches. And the door—unembossed—so smooth that the spirit of God's mercy slipped down to the frozen earth. "So how ought I to live?! How ought I to live, according to you?!"

"You should open yourself to the Lord," said the door. "Go inside and you will see him enter!"

"But I see only cold and darkness."

"Because you are blind. He enters into people's hearts."

"The hearts of these?" . . . Several ordinary eyes passed over us without interest. "Foreigners! What do you want with us?" Cold streamed from the interior as if there was more inside than outside. I said: "Let's get away."

And so it happened that we went back in the direction of the main street and could not fail to see the ostentatious sign "Restaurant Europa." The Restaurant Europa spoke our language.

"We'll eat here whatever it costs," said Tomas.

"Hey?" I said as we were already pushing through the glass doors, "Do you have the bill that Romu gave us?"

"Romu?"

"You know, Romu."

"Aha."

Inside we were caught off guard by the old familiar dimness and cold. We had expected an embalming warmth, in which tiredness would spread into all corners of the body while the soft smell of food ascended. But a State of Emergency prevailed. The restaurant could even be closed.

That is what we said to ourselves as we went further into the darkened room where tables without tablecloths yawned with emptiness. "It's up to you; do whatever you think best," said the dirty curtain half obscuring the entrance.

"It's dreadful here," I said. For some incomprehensible reason no light came from the chandeliers. In the corner, in front of a black partition separating off the remaining part of the room, sat the only guests. The windows were so blacked out that very little could be made out. No more than that the guests were sitting in overcoats and sheepskin hats and that the Formica tabletop in front of them was covered with lemonade bottles but no glasses. A chill ran down my spine. My rucksack became heavy and I was amazed that I had carried it so far. We wound between the tables.

"Don't go there!" I shouted suddenly. "Tomas, I beg you, don't go there!" A terrible animal fear clutched at my heart. Tomas turned and stared at me. The seated citizens also raised their heads. "Don't go there, I'm frightened."

I retreated quickly. Tomas also came back, although he didn't know why. I regained my nerve a little. I remained standing in the shaft of light that was falling through a large window. Here I felt safe. "Let's sit here," I pointed shakily to the nearest table.

"What on earth's the matter?" said Tomas.

We sat down. "I don't know."

A waitress in sweater and mittens came up and furiously pounded on the table. "It's forbidden to sit at this table! You must move!"

What could we do? The last hot meal we had eaten had been our Christmas carp. And our backpacks weighed us down. "You're an unbelievable bitch," I retorted shakily in her stupid face and she tapped her forehead. Then she went away.

There was now no light falling on our table and once again I felt some evil presence. I thought I could see the burning end of a cigarette and somebody's shadow behind the partition. The tension emanating from that place meant that it could only be him.

"Don't you think that someone is standing there?"

"No. Can you see someone?"

"Maybe."

"Do you think that he knew where we were going?"

"Leave it!" That was just like Tomas. He could talk with me for hours about the color of the eyes of spirits that he did not believe in. On the other hand I was grateful to him for not laughing at my weakness. He overlooked it with perfect tact.

It was just that now I was absolutely sure he was standing there. But I didn't care any more. In this inhospitable darkness I simply lacked the will to resist fate. Everything here was so depressing. And if I had moved I would have lost the last vestiges of warmth I still possessed.

It was really quite interesting: observing what would become of us. The waitress came back holding a plate of cold food in each hand. On one trembled a small hillock of meat jelly, and on the other a few small pieces of cheese hopelessly yearned for closer contact with a spot of sausage and a little heap of vegetables. It was a miracle that the dishes were not covered in drift-ice.

"This one or that one!?" the waitress signaled grimly. We timidly chose the second. The waitress added three small bread-rolls.

The plate gave the impression of a cold foreign body on the smooth tabletop. The table had the same effect in the large room, and extensive areas on the plate gaped with emptiness. I tried a little sausage. But as I bit at it my mouth filled with icy water. Then I hesitantly chewed and at each new bite more and more water ran into my mouth. The citizens at the furthest table stood up and slowly surrounded us. I tasted the cheese. There were five citizens and the cheese was unpleasantly salty. I tried to swallow it quickly. This time, however, the tempo of destiny and the tempo of my stomach were not synchronized because at the very moment I attempted to swallow, a heavy hand grabbed my shoulder and I, instead of swallowing, screamed out: "No! No, please no!"

III

They took us out into a deserted courtyard. Their faces reeked of crudeness, but the everyday sort. I stopped being afraid of them.

One wore blue workman's trousers soiled with plaster. He shouted something incomprehensible at us. We tried to follow all their commands. It wasn't quite possible. Another three were more desiccated than the first. The oldest had a face covered by a layer of red pimples. Half old men and half wooden figurines. The wood that remained was indestructible. The fifth was a young man—almost a boy. In our country kids like him used to straddle motorcycles after village dances. Between his lips was a cigarette.

The sixth had been standing behind the partition and behind everything. But he didn't show himself in the courtyard.

I was ashamed of my display of weakness. The hand that had gripped my shoulder had belonged to the boy. Now he smiled at me maliciously.

They led us to the other side of the courtyard. The frame

of my backpack struck me on the knee. I stopped to swing it onto my back, but one of the men shouted at me.

"Idiots! I could follow them more easily if I had it on my back." But I shouldn't have said it. They looked me up and down dangerously. I realized that these people always sensed when somebody didn't take them seriously enough. "Don't do anything to draw attention to yourself, or they may separate us," the thought flashed through my mind.

In a den at the end of the courtyard was something like an office. First they stepped into a short passage that had no proper floor and was only separated from the yard by a single window. To the left this opened into a room. The man in the workman's trousers motioned us to the entrance. We tried to act in a disciplined way; to such an extent, in fact, that we didn't even look at each other. The cracked wood of the floor under my feet met my eyes. I knew that Tomas was looking at the same thing.

On the soiled table stood a bottle and beside it two people were sitting on chairs. The third lay on a straw mattress by the wall. There was nothing else in the room apart from a bulb in the ceiling, a black switch, a lamp, and a small stove where a fire was smoldering. Next to the bottle lay a crumpled notebook. The walls were made of unpainted hardboard.

Of those who had brought us only the boy with the cigarette came inside. He smiled triumphantly. I was glad that the one with the pimply face had stayed outside. Not that he was necessarily so bad, but his ugliness embarrassed me. I felt that when I looked at him I was involuntarily injuring him.

The man on the mattress sat up and sized us up coolly. He had round, feline features with a covert harshness. The black shadows on his shaven jaw completed the picture.

One of the men sitting by the table got up and pushed his chair toward me. This created a tricky situation for me: there were no other chairs in the room and I didn't know how he would take it if I sat down in his place. Embarrassed,

I remained standing. At this the second got up, grabbed me by the sleeve and roughly pushed me into the chair. I felt a burning and inextinguishable hatred for him.

As long as I had been standing I had still kept some grip on myself, but now I was completely in their power. The chair sucked away my last drops of self-confidence. "And what about Tomas? Won't they make Tomas sit down?" I thought.

They gripped him by the shoulder and pointed at the free part of the mattress as if to say: "You have a place there, you little fool; how come you don't know it?" He looked at me in terror. The mattress. How much would the mattress bear?

They took our passports and scribbled something in the notebook. The backpacks were slung against the wall. The lanky one who had seated me so roughly walked up and down the room several times. I imagined squashing him into a messy pulp between my palms. That long neck with the rhomboid head, grotesquely small above the broad shoulders. That self-assured smile. Swine!

Tomas was now sitting opposite me. The boy with the cigarette sat down beside him. "Parlez-vous français?" he tried us. (I think that it was the only phrase he knew.) "Nu, nu française," I answered modestly and tried to sound admiring. "Nu?" the boy responded with satisfaction.

My eyes met Tomas's, which were unaccustomedly soft in his now red face. His bottom touched the bottoms of his guards. Drops of sweat were running down his temples.

Cathead gave a few brusque orders. Lanky took a deep breath and pounced: "Speak Slovensky?!" We gasped. To hear a familiar language sound so foreign. "Da," I answered in the local language.

"What you do here?" he said.

"We want to get to the mountains. Mountains. Mountaineering."

"Now?! What about this baggage!" he pointed at the backpacks. "Unpack!"

We didn't know whether we were allowed to get up. "Unpack?"

But Lanky had already flung himself at my backpack and begun to unstrap it. He managed it unexpectedly quickly; he immediately lifted it and turned it upside down. The carefully packed contents spilled out on the floor: clothes, food, the ax clinked.

"And what is this?"

"It's an ax. For wood."

"For wood? Second one!" he pointed peevishly. Tomas hurried over to his rucksack. I too stood up and tried to pull the last few things out of mine. But Lanky was no longer interested, "Who have you been in contact with?" he said. "Contact?" "Contacting! Talk!" shouted Lanky with his ugly rhomboid head.

"The Cudeans," the name flashed through my mind. "What if they know about them? But no. We only met them by accident."

"We don't know anybody here. We are going to the mountains. Mountains," I said.

It didn't look as if he understood. He scribbled something down in the notebook for a moment and then let fly some word. When we didn't understand he repeated it twice. Suddenly the sounds came together and the result was the Russian word "Wherefrom?" We told him our full home addresses and he checked them against our passports. He looked questioningly at his superior. What next?

The situation in the room was slowly changing. The man who had vacated his seat for me at the beginning now got up and walked around our things inquisitively. Cathead crossed the room with feverish steps and drank deeply. A peculiar person. I kept having to look at him. I couldn't decide whether I liked him or not. "Couldn't these jokers stoke the heating up properly?" I thought.

We stood by the pile of emptied out things. Their eyes drilled into us with a learned brutality. Why couldn't they behave decently to us even for a moment? Did we have to be assumed guilty just because we were suspected of something?

The abortive Slovak turned to us again. "Contact?" he screamed with his last strength. His knowledge of the language was probably only a facade. Maybe he once worked as a customs officer or a conductor. Bastard. In appearance he bore a striking resemblance to one of the older beanpoles from our street. That one had a seriously sick wife and went for walks with a monstrously ugly mutt. During the war he had flown in the Australian airforce.

"Nu contact. Mountains."

"Mountains?"

An incomprehensible debate broke out. The guys in charge of our things discovered the carton of cigarettes and the packets vanished into pockets. One of the two axes also disappeared under a jacket.

"Pack it up!" ordered Lanky with distaste.

The end came unexpectedly quickly. We packed hurriedly and willingly. Cathead said something to the others. The black shadows shone on his face.

When we had packed up Lanky came up to us conspiratorially. They were all suddenly conspirators and slightly embarrassed: "Rubber?"

"Rubber?" Our eyes widened in bafflement. We grasped no more than that maybe we were no longer in danger.

"Primeros, Preservativ," a second came to his aid. Everyone looked at us in expectation.

"We primeros?"

"Da."

"We nu primeros. Don't have."

They hung their heads in disappointment. "Nu primeros?"

"Unfortunately."

For a moment it was quiet. Then Cathead nodded toward

the door and threw us our passports. We left, continuously reassuring ourselves that we had understood correctly. In front of the door Lanky stopped us. "You cannot stay," he said. "You will go to the station! Tomorrow a train will go. You understand?!" He looked into our eyes. We nodded.

They let us through the doors into the courtyard, where it was quiet. The sixth, who was behind it all, remained hidden. The boy came out with us and led us toward the open passageway. Suddenly his behavior was friendly. At the end of the passageway he reached into his packet and pulled out a blue bill. "Rubber, " he said, and longingly gazed at the sidepockets of our backpacks, which had not been unstrapped.

"Nu rubber," we repeated in ingratiating tones.

"Nu?" He sadly put the bill back in a pocket in which our cigarettes glinted.

We set off along the graying street. I looked at my watch. It was half past three. In the sky, which had welcomed us with the dawn, there now hung dry, omnipresent clouds. But the cold was not receding.

We went back as far as the edge of the square where the church with the iron gate stood. The monotonous intonement of prayer reached us. We realized that this was not the direction in which we wanted to go. We stood there helplessly. The tones of prayer grew faint and we felt like weeping because we had to return to the station and because Jesus Christ was born to be crucified for the sins of humankind.

"It's high time to lose ourselves in the mountains," said Tomas.

"High time."

We walked through the town streets as through the ravines of a darkening valley. Below us somebody's feet clattered over the uneven pavement. Above us the silenced hillsides, strangely exhausted by the holiday, prepared for sleep. We moved on pace by pace. But in the north an iron grille was already sliding from east to west and threatening to close the town before we could reach its edge. We quickened our steps in the fear that it would cut us off. We marched with all our strength and the sweat was pouring from us; on each side cracked masonry flickered by and disappeared. Far to the west sounded the warning trumpets of twilight. Once, then once again. At last we overcame the pull of the earth and began to float. Two strangers sailing like the favorites of hell through ever empty streets. We left the station and the Restaurant Europa behind us in a great arc; we flew over the representative zone of the town and we aimed, across two previously unknown crossroads, at the place where we believed that the North-South Road opened into the north. The labyrinth of houses was now replaced by uniform lines of factory walls. At a depth that had ceased to be measurable, avenues of trees swayed and a double line of barbed wire unrolled forward along the nape of a wooden fence. Tangled in it was a dangling extinguished shadow that belonged to the body of the man with the rhomboid head who had wounded my "I." His long arms and legs were everywhere visible and his broken trunk, gnawed by birds, shone black and white. Huge manufacturing plants yawned with emptiness to left and right. And in their forecourts, as far as we could see, there was no one. The wind whistled: only a few hundred meters separated us from the edge of the town. For the third time, and the most penetrating, sounded the trumpets of twilight. We alighted in front of a disconnected caravan, behind which the North-South road ran into lumpy clay fields. On the other side a pocket-sized village crouched in the dark. Along an unseen country road between the town and the village luminous specters of armored trucks glided across the horizon. (The soldiers were vacuum-sealing the town.) From the caravan came the soft affectionate strumming tones of a guitar. Our knees buckled beneath us. Too late—too late for everything. We eased off our backpacks and sat down on the frozen ground beside wheels long past service. It was inexpressibly warm and untouched, just as in the beginning. The sky was soaked in ink and the area had submerged itself in darkness. We had failed to reach the longed-for mountains . . . trala tralala trara tra tra tra la la.

"Jesus!" Tomas started, "what if the State of Emergency means a curfew after a certain hour?" he whispered.

"You're right. It usually does mean that. What'll they do with us if they catch us?"

(I too was talking in a subdued voice—no more than the immobilized surroundings could bear.)

"What would they do with us? Shoot us on sight. We ought to get somewhere fast."

We pulled ourselves up. The guitar suddenly stopped, but this was apparently nothing to do with us. A little longer and we would have fallen asleep where we sat. Now we were on our feet again. Unconsciously I touched myself on the parts where one sits.

We could see into the fields over the rusty connecting rod. Around the shining vehicles flickered the silhouettes of people taking up firing positions.

"Is there any point in going to the station?"

"No."

"Where then?"

"There's no sense in anything but the Cudeans."

"Quickly then."

This time we didn't manage to fly up. On the contrary, for a little while I felt as if we were walking on the spot. As if the pavement was caving in; the walls were leaning forwards.

I was reflecting on our goal of returning to the Cudeans. People are not usually generous twice. One must take that into account and not expose friends to pressure. Stupid town. Stupid North-South Road, so narrow and so long.

Nobody was walking anywhere; the street lighting was off. All that was left was darkness, fear, and direction. Shots could ring out again or anything else might happen.

"Do you really think that you're the one choosing the direction of your steps?" said my skeptical "I." I did not reply. "This whole day is like a deflected line and you have been led along it," the voice continued. "First you wanted to get to the mountains. Then—when that didn't work—you said you would stay here. After that you wanted to go to the mountains again. But when you had the opportunity you didn't take the shortest route. You wandered through the town. In the end it turned out you felt you had to get to the mountains. And now: yet again you have to go somewhere. But this time you really must. You always want to involve your will in things. As if it were possible to turn away from the road that has been prepared."

The North-South Road had become a channel sloping down toward us. "Try it! Try it!" called the sidestreets leading God knows where. I ran to the nearest and the narrowest. It led away along a mild slope. It was almost entirely dark there and sometimes I passed the trunks of trees. The ice-covered pavement rose ever more steeply. It was rapidly becoming a sharp climb. I ran up the street with all my strength and when running became impossible I leaned on my hands and clambered up on all fours. The slope was now at a good sixty degrees and the angle increased continuously. I groped for the chinks between the cobblestones and clung on tenaciously. My feet slipped off and I hung stretched out on an almost vertical wall. I realized that I couldn't get any further. Something snapped: I felt the snow and ice beneath me, flashing by at enormous speed. Something heaped up below and pushed me a little higher. Then I slowly slid back down to the place from which I had run. I became paralyzed. The town made a threatening step toward me. Once again I remembered the way it all had been when I had encountered it at sunrise.

"Livie. It's a beautiful name. How did you come by it?" I asked.

"How do I know," she whispered, "to whom I owe my name?" and met my eyes with an unexpectedly challenging smile, which said "You ask me very nonsensical questions, sir! Do you by any chance mean to say that you like me?!"

The self-confident femininity of the gesture caught me unaware. I realized that I had been wide of the mark. When would I stop confusing tenderness with childishness?

Livie was now sitting opposite me, wrapped from the waist down in a warm woolen blanket, and looking like a woman who wanted to play a game. Yes, I should have realized that opposite me I had a flesh-and-blood, courageous (if at first shy and anxious to please) woman and not a porcelain doll blushing mindlessly.

Simeonu came in wearing tracksuit, sweater, and bathrobe. "So it's not possible to leave the town. Well, I thought so. They have vacuum-sealed the town," he mumbled in German.

"I was just saying," I tried to wriggle out of the difficult situation, "that Livie is a beautiful name, but rather unusual in Bohemia. Is it common here?" Simeonu thought for a moment and looked at Livie. "Even here it's not so common. It's occasionally used." They smiled at each other.

"I understand," I said.

German words—those I understood and those I didn't know—had once again grown together with the foundation of our brief communications. They were ultimately no more than symbols while the ground on which the scene was played was common to us both. For this reason I could understand what was hidden behind them and for this reason I was able to speak through them and say what I wished.

Simeonu sat down. The room swam in a dimness to which our many-layered clothing added a mysterious touch.

At the sides loomed the outlines of the objects close to us. I trembled. It did not fit together: so much home and so much cold.

"My wife is bringing tea in a moment," said Simeonu, apologetically. "We are only allowed one electric plate."

"But really . . ." Once again I realized how enormously kind they were. I suddenly knew that I myself would not have been able to manage it: to welcome two foreigners twice in the same day without a shadow of a second thought, without the briefest hesitation. Without fear, if for nothing else, then for their scrap of privacy, clearly the last value that remained to them. Slowly the moment we had rung at their door receded. It had seemed an eternity before Simeonu had opened the door with a decisive but uneasy movement. Inscribed in his face and gestures was the knowledge of everything that might come in from the outside here.

Tomas now dashed in from the kitchen. "I've seen their ration tickets," he called out in Czech. "Just imagine, they get an allocation of a kilo of meat a month. Do you understand? A kilo of meat."

Simeonu and Livie gazed at his lips in fright.

"We are staggered at your meat ration," I explained.

To my surprise Simeonu gave a hearty laugh, like an enlightened patriot who knows that a national specialty is particularly amusing to foreigners. How could he manage it? Tomas and I had the bodies of sportsmen, almost affluent in their health. Really he ought to hate us.

Nothing. Tomas settled himself between us like a log. He looked around swaggeringly to see who would start to speak, and when no one did, he took up the task himself. "Well, Martin," he addressed me in front of everybody and I could only wait and see how big a gaffe he would make, "Have you been been telling Mlle. Livie something sweet?"

I felt the need to rocket myself through the ceiling and into the universe. "What do you mean? Something sweet?" I retorted coldly.

"Just some sweet nothings that we tell pretty mademoi-selles." Heat swept over me. I shook my head uncompre-hendingly. Perhaps the others didn't take it so seriously. Probably they didn't register it at all. But I, on the other hand, had the impression that all my efforts to present myself with dignity had been ruined. I wanted to say some-thing very nasty. But a penetrating ring of the bell bit deep into all our breasts. And sucked there a long time. We froze. Then the father rose and combed the room with terrified eyes searching for a place where he could hide us. But the dresser cried, "I am too narrow . . . and it would be foolish-ness, foolishness!" The bookcase fidgeted strangely: "Why are you staring at me?" And the table simply avoided his gaze, and so the father remained alone. He set off as if on a long pilgrimage and Livie too stood up while we pressed ourselves yet deeper into our upholstered armchairs.

The mother came in with her hands on her apron, and stood there mute; from the very beginning she had struck me as the least independent of the whole family: she was apprehensive and in decisive moments waited to see what the others would do. I already knew her questioning eyes, full of dependence.

Voices sounded from the hall and Livie smiled exhausted-ly. I used the opportunity to turn to Tomas: "Don't even think about talking such bullshit ever again!" I whispered angrily. "Don't even think about it!" Tomas stared at me in surprise. "You take everything too seriously," he said sadly, and he was right.

Only the mirror he held up to me in being right sudden-ly appalled me. And I was gripped by a brutal hunger—I saw myself through the gate of my empty stomach: serious for ever and ever—serious as a belly that is bottomless and even when filled keeps on croaking a guttural song that it detests. And high in my throat I felt mother earth, not that great globe but the black soil that is below us, survives us, and is in us—that soil which, if I crumble it in my palms and put it in my mouth, will do me good. But below me there was only the carpet, beneath it the parquet, and on the window the alien frost. Tomas's grief, wounding (because correct), and my longing to eat the earth. "Livie, graceful Livie, do you think the same of me?"

"Was it Petresku, father?" she asked. "It was Petresku, wasn't it? What did he want?" She was speaking her language; I only made out the word "Petresku" twice and guessed the rest. It struck me that if they dragged her father away, I would be closer to her. She would surely put herself in my hands and I would use my prestige as a foreigner and bring her father back to her. I needed more space to express myself to her somehow, and the perverted nature of such thoughts did not horrify me. After all, her father was here, alive and well. Why shouldn't I imagine how it might turn out in other circumstances?!

"There are no other circumstances," countered my skeptical "I." "Something that requires circumstances that don't exist in order to exist simply doesn't exist."

"But you must admit that if, for example, they dragged her father away . . . "

"Don't blaspheme!"

"I only wanted to explain that . . ."

"You have to prove who you are, under real circumstances!"

"But I still think . . ." "Where is Andrei?" I said aloud. Only in doing so I interrupted Simeonu, cutting into his first, still unarticulated word. He stopped short as if he was hesitating about which thread of the conversation to pursue, and in the end he waved his hand in no particular direction. It meant "Andrei away." And it wordlessly implied "I know where." His original plan of communication had, however, been lost beyond recall.

"Livie," Tomas let himself be heard in the ensuing silence, "would you show me your medicine cabinet?"

"Why do you need to see her medicine cabinet?" I inquired in Czech.

"I have a splitting headache."

I scrutinized him searchingly. There really was a strange film on his forehead and his eyes, and it had not been there just a moment before. Pain radiated from him. Embarrassed by his inability to put it into words, Tomas left the room with Livie and I stayed by myself with the father and mother. Who was it then who had rung the bell? I looked questioningly into the father's grave face. In front of me stood another cup of tea. The tea was tepid, almost cold, and my fingertips too were chill. A hopeless silence. The feeble lightbulb cast long shadows through the room.

"Some difficulty?" I asked finally.

"No, you needn't be afraid," smiled the father. His serious air had disappeared and it was pleasant to believe him—not to worry about anything and to believe. "A neighbor visited me," he continued patiently, "to see how we were. Yesterday the Inspector for Electricity Saving was apparently looking around the building. For this." And Simeonu pointed at the ceiling, again with the peculiar self-ironizing humor that almost everyone here possessed. I imagined my own father in his place: a wise, serious man, almost the same age. They even had the same thick network of crow's-feet around their eyes. It was only that self-ironizing humor. . . . The limits of desperation had been stretched so far that there remained only laughter. To laugh and laugh . . . over this hopelessness.

"What does it mean: the Inspector for Electricty Saving?"

"It's a very bad man," said Simeonu as if he were telling children a fairy tale. "With police power. For example, if that lightbulb here and the one by the door were both on at the same time, it would be a breach of regulations. Or an electric plate and that lightbulb."

"That means that you can either cook or have light?"

"Basically yes. Our country is in a very bad energy situation. And it's only the beginning of winter." An ironical grimace. Really, even his forehead resembled my father's. Only Simeonu's was a little narrower. More southern features. And longer hair. "But the reality is not so strict as the regulations," he went on. "You saw for yourself. We cooked and had the light on. Look . . ."

I hadn't even noticed that Mirela had gone out. Now she was placing a plate of beans in front of me. She looked at me questioningly: "And your friend?"

"Tomas!" I called, "There's a plate of beans for you here."

"Beans?" muttered Tomas from the hall.

"I'm telling you: beans for both of us."

"Hm."

At last he came in—indifferently, heavy-footed and as if deliberately sunk in another world, the world of pain. His difficulties infused me with unexpected strength. I was revived: I felt like dancing through the room and onto Tomas's stooped back. I grabbed the plate and gulped it down with the mash. At first I was careful, but then I stopped caring about anything—I was breaking it rapidly and grinding it in my teeth: beans and porcelain—it was exactly what I needed.

"What can we do for you? I mean for your people, your country?"

Silence.

"Idiot, you yourself want to be excluded from their game. From every game," my skeptical "I" flung in my face.

"I will show you something," said the father and stood up. It was not an answer to my question. At least not a direct answer.

"What sort of thing do you imagine we could do for them?" said Tomas, once again puzzled. "I don't know about you, but I have enough worries of my own: my head aches, I've eaten about three spoonfuls of beans, Livie doesn't love me . . . "

"Leave that out . . . "

The father had not rebuffed my question but only circumvented it. He laid some kind of manuscript in the middle of the table. Everything had to . . . and therefore fell silent. Livie stood with her face turned to the window—even more emaciated, it seemed to me . . . yes, at that moment I seemed to hear her heart beating. And if it had all been a film then background music, the slightly anticipatory tones of the "Marseillaise" or another heroic march, would have approached from the distance. But it was no film. I knew that this table here was far from being an ordinary wooden table—and that perhaps at just this moment it was one of the most important tables in the Country. Although there was no march. Tons and tons of matter were here heaped on top of each other. The resistance of people dug into the ground.

"These are the demands with which the workers in the big plants will be going on strike tomorrow."

An awkward silence set in during which we gazed at the spread papers, not knowing what to do or say. The father too was dismayed—he saw that he had gone too far. His turmoil was palpable: his inner modesty and natural need to boast. The latter finally prevailed: "I teach languages at the largest secondary school here," he said. "My brother works in one of the plants. Before Christmas he came to me and asked me to put the demands together for them."

"We've got ourselves into a regular hornets' nest," commented Tomas.

I kept quiet. I had no idea what attitude I should take. I should probably have said: "Please read us the demands, professor," but nothing on earth would have forced the words from my lips. At the same time I did not want to drive the old man into starting to read without encouragement: the poor wretch was horribly embarrassed as the letters he had written down with such dedication now flashed in front of us like beans on a plate. The letters that could have . . . what exactly?

"The big plants: are they those production halls on the edge of the town?"

"Yes, those ones."

In front of me rose the landscape of factory forecourts and warehouses. All my life I had cultivated the idea of revolt and now . . . and now it was indecently near. What would the workers eat during the strike? I wondered. And what if their demands were not met? "It doesn't seem possible to me that the regime here would yield an inch," I said. "Even if it wanted. Even if it wanted."

"Our demands are not so fundamental as you may think," said Simeonu almost apologetically, "we are asking, for example, for buses to be allocated to take workers to the surrounding villages after work."

"Workers here go to and from work on foot," Livie contributed heatedly. "It's inhuman. Some of them, if they don't get a lift, have to walk eighteen kilometers a day."

I gazed out of the window. There—somewhere below— ran the roads and paths tramped by the heavy steps of workmen making for the fields. I saw the workers walking in the morning rain. I saw them, shadowy and exuding an identical smell, standing in the corridor of the train. In the overflowing stations. Pitch-black clothes enveloped their bodies and I couldn't imagine them getting undressed at home and making love to their women under feather quilts. I couldn't even pull off their boots before they went to bed; nor their trousers nor their overcoats.

"Or setting up a factory canteen," continued Livie. "The workers now depend on cold meals they bring from home. And nobody listens. A year ago a few employees complained that they lived too far away. Provisional barracks were built for them on the edge of the town and they were moved there with their families. Their farms were razed to the ground."

"How appalling," I thought.

"That's how it is," nodded the father. "These are the problems we have at the moment. Maybe the most common demand is to ease the law against marriages with fewer than two children." He spoke in a very small voice, as if he were tired to death by the subject of which he was talking. Perhaps it was only now that he realized the insuperable distance from freedom. "This law . . . it is a disgrace."

But Livie did not share his exhaustion. "A woman who has fewer than two children is exposed to continuous pressure," she burst out. "A district inspector comes to her family and admonishes her to conform. If that doesn't help she is sent for humiliating medical examinations. It is . . . "

My eyes drilled though her. She blushed. I hung my head and buried my gaze under the table. I had nothing encouraging to say to her.

The mother came in and came to each of us offering cookies. She probably didn't know what we were talking about; at this moment her already creased face exuded an inexpressible contentment. If she hadn't been so tall she might still, even now, have been a sweet little woman. Her height, however, made her seem tiresome.

Livie was smiling helplessly. I took a large biscuit and went to the window; Tomas followed me a moment later and then at last Livie, although she remained a step behind us. We were nibbling our cookies and looking through the window into a space full of raw white darkness. All the time I felt that Livie was waiting for me to say something. But everything that occurred to me in German was either a statement of something banal or a foolish conversational cliché. I realized we were condemned to slide over the surface of words— two exiles from the womb of the communicable.

I returned to the table and to the father's papers, which lay there untouched. The father had his head in his hands and the last sentence that he had uttered was rolling on the table in front of him like a curved liverwurst. "This law . . . it is a disgrace."

Tomas picked up one of the papers and looked at it with reverence. "After all . . . they could meet such demands."

"I would still like to add to them," the father started slowly, "that when my children were small . . . I didn't spoil them . . . but"—he was forcing it out uneasily, as if still looking for the right words—"they were given everything they needed. But if I had children now . . . as a secondary-school professor . . . and if I didn't have a sister in the country . . . I would be afraid that they would go hungry. I would like to write that."

He looked at us questioningly and I could see the idea growing in him. He no longer needed us for it; it blossomed into a minute mournful flower in the meadows of his inner struggles. And it was no longer a question of workers, of politics, of the nation. It concerned him—and therefore the world.

But: demands presented, strike prepared, document drafted!

"Bang, bang, bang," the window rattled. "Bang, bang, wake up! You take it seriously until you're up against it! Bang and crash! The journey's long, the journey's dark, shame and fear! Provoke them, bully them, dream up non-sense! Grandmother's steps, brother in jail, model house-wife, kicks in the head. First children, second children, hocus-pocus, dried-up bread, foreigners!"

Foreigners.

"When I tell the authorities this, they ought to give it all up. Everybody ought to give it all up." And when we were silent, he went on: "It's a question of the possibility of living according to your own lights. But when you have nothing to eat, when your family has nothing to eat, when in the evening you don't have enough light to read by. The worst thing is that here even the poverty isn't your own. It's some-one else's poverty planted on you."

"It's easy to consider it," I thought. "But how does he want to do it? Does he really want to go to his brother and tell him to add this point?" I wondered if he really thought so and to my surprise I discovered that a gray dove had settled on his head. The dove softly shielded the back of his head and certainly warmed him through his hair. They were so united (those two) that I began to feel out of place beside them.

"It's happened to him again," whispered Livie.

No, it was no longer my business. It would be better to go away somewhere or at least to the next room, but I couldn't. And it was also impossible to stay. We were sitting around the table: between us poor Simeonu as if he were afflicted by a peculiar disease. I was afraid that he would bend his head and the dove would fall or vanish. If he didn't add what he had said to the paper then it would vanish. Or if he raised his voice. There had already been too much anger and struggle. In front of me there opened up a wide white path. The exhaustion of everything. I lie down in the snow at the end of the path. At the beginning of the path. Nothing matters any more and so I can savor everything. Only I. He and It. Close to the ground it is warm; I drink in downy bird-feathers through the cracks of my hair. I am victor over my own defeat.

The dove rested silently as if above the heads of two men in an old picture.

"Livie, please tell your mother that the cookies were good," said Tomas.

IN THE NAME OF THE DOVE

I

FIRST, IT WAS GETTING LATE. I SAID THAT I WOULD DELIVER Simeonu's demands to wherever he wanted. I rolled out my sleeping bag on the carpet. In that moment the room drew close around me, something that never happens on visits. I felt that as soon as I lay down it would speak to me confidentially.

Simeonu went out and the dove floated down under the surface of things. A peculiar determination and assurance took root in me. This was now my fixed place. From here I could go anywhere.

I slowly unpacked my sleeping things and laid them out on the cold floor. Livie was standing in the doorway. Just like me, she probably could not grasp that the long day was at an end. From my vantage point I could see her legs.

Sounds of home were also coming from the bedroom. Livie was wearing a dressing-gown. Her calves were shining above her thick socks. Later, they would shine on my path at a time when Livie was already lost forever.

Yes, Livie will vanish. The cold waters will close over her and she will not be. Not even her thin face.

"Well then . . . until tomorrow. Goodnight."

I stretched out at full length; the tension in my bowels and inner organs eased. A river of warmth flooded my body.

Most warming of all was the consciousness of my future journey.

Tomas fell asleep immediately. A pale light from the hallway fell across him through the half-closed door. Without it we would have been surrounded by darkness. For a moment I wanted to open the window and lean out. It was a wish I could allow myself, now that I was already ensconced in my feather sleeping bag.

The silhouette of a bookcase loomed from the wall and immediately above my head there was a shelf and a candlestick. My legs were extended under the table; these shapes wrapped themselves around my body like some exceptionally airy clothing. Or like pillars protruding from my body across eternity.

"You shouldn't leave me right above your head," said the candlestick. "I've never fallen yet but maybe tonight I'm going to fall and hurt you."

"Why fall tonight of all nights?" I wondered. "Do you have something against me?"

"I have nothing against you. I just sense that blood is going to flow. And your head is nearest."

I slid further under the table. "You frighten me," I whispered timidly. "I'd rather that you told me something ancient and beautiful."

"It wouldn't be so ancient or so beautiful. It's the story of a human quest that has led back to its starting point. And of yet another human quest. Only sometimes brass hands sound in the wind. And of all parts of a tree the roots are the most important."

"I would be a liar if I said I understood you," I answered. "My mother is of Jewish origin and my father isn't. I've always been trying to discover the Jew in myself. I meet it at every step but I never could catch it. It's like a puppy chasing its own tail."

"If you were a Jew at heart, the tail would stop your mouth. But I want to talk about myself. I'm nothing now but a family memento, a reminder of roots. That's my problem."

"They've just forgotten to take you down—it's not so bad for you here. Where I come from we would have exhibited you as a curiosity."

In the short silence that followed it seemed to me that the candlestick might break into weeping and I was flooded with an inexpressible grief. It raised its overflowing, blackened, red-and-yellow eyes toward the ceiling and tears of brass coursed down.

"It's not really so bad." I tried to comfort it, and myself too. "Some things endure in the world until the puppy catches its tail."

I was fast losing control of myself. From the center of the bookcase a distant country path stretched toward me. The first two steps along it had already been accomplished. They had been taken by the goblin from the train and I was amazed at how sharply they led uphill through the land of yellow clay. The goblin turned back to me with the air of a wanton angel who had absolute control over me. It took another five steps along the path that water had gouged down to the stone. It turned again—this time commandingly. I set off after it. It walked a few paces in front of me and swayed grotesquely from side to side. I took the fact that I was following as a piece of voluntary foolery, as a consequence of a stubbornness so coquettish as to be irresistible. The sweat stood out on my forehead.

The goblin toddled tirelessly on. At last—breathless, since the path was very steep—I came to a standstill. It turned around and I tried to win it over with a good-natured grimace—the same grimace that had inspired its sweet puzzlement in the train corridor. This time, however, it looked dismissive and severe. I didn't try anything similar again. Even so it was mightily displeased, and its enmity was increasingly obvious in its pestering commands. On each side were plowed fields and the path wound between them. Suddenly we were standing at the top of a drop. There was a sandy terrace beneath us and in the distance Prague lay spread out. The goblin came up to me. Its head was bent so that I could not see its eyes. I realized its intention and swung at it wildly. But it jumped at me from behind and grabbed me round the legs. I was standing at the very edge of the rock. I raised my right arm and with all my strength struck behind me—I felt I'd got it hard in the head and neck. But even though my blows were precise and strong, my toes were edging toward the precipice. I went berserk and experienced the horror and pleasure of hammering at a live child's body. Yet I could not avoid falling, for the goblin was the embodiment of a higher imperative force. My feet slipped from under me and I fell on my backside, which slid to the edge and beyond. I managed to deal a final furious blow to the diabolical creature—a blow which flattened its childish nose. Then I flew away like a shred of cloth.

Slowly I picked myself out of the sand. Not far from me—under a half-leafless apple tree—two pilgrims were sitting. Both surveyed me without interest, and this drew me to them. I came up closer. One—a grayhead with long-flowing beard and a pilgrim staff—smiled bitterly. He was like a saint from old paintings, and only from there, since he had no substance. The second one had an unapproachable air. He was a handsome, well-grown man of flesh and blood. As they sat, elbow to elbow, they absently warmed each other's hands in their mutually extended palms.

"Where are you going" I asked simply. I wondered where I had found such presence of mind.

"We are abandoning Prague," sighed the elder man, and gave a sob of grief.

"We are getting out of Prague," added the younger one harshly.

"There is no longer any place for us there," continued the elder.

"It's a shit-hole. A complete shit-hole." thundered the

younger. The elder cast his eyes down in a tortured gesture at these shocking words. But then he realized that I was involved as well and raised them again. "Don't listen to him. He is cruel and evil," he said.

"And he is old and worthless," retorted the cruel and evil one. A peculiar asymmetry. It would not have been possible to respond with "And he is cruel, evil, and young." The youth of the cruel and evil one could hardly be regarded as a negative attribute.

They went on warming their hands, palm to palm, and grief made them one. As I stood before them our surroundings became ever more indistinct. Only Prague, which had been spread out in the distance, seemed close beside us. I could reach out and touch its tapered towers.

"People who are the same are dead because one can easily replace another," continued the older pilgrim. "Their life is like the buzzing of a fly in the noonday sun. Where there is no difference, there can be no story. For this reason we must depart. We are the double axis of all stories."

"Fuck off and stuff your blatherings up your ass; fuck off, I tell you," blazed the younger, radiating menace. Immediately, however, he realized that this was absurd and he calmed down. "Or I'll smash your teeth in," he added in moderate tones. As he spoke he started to resemble the elder until they were as like as two pins and his face dissolved. The old man rose to his feet and we two stood alone in a flood of silver beard. "We are dead," he whispered. "And immobility is hard on our heels, which is worse than the worst demon." His eyes burned like two setting suns. "And by the way," he went on, "the toothbrush you've brought with you isn't good enough. It has an unnecessarily long handle and the bristle density is one point two when the optimal density is one point five bristles per square millimeter." He stepped back and smiled craftily. Suddenly, however, he gave me a look of reprimand. "Be good enough to explain what is the meaning of this," he said, and pointed behind him. There stood the goblin from the train—that charming creature, stooped like a puppet. Instead of a nose it had a bloody pancake and I recognized my blows in other bloody stains. The little girl fixed devoted and childish eyes on me. I realised that my action was irreparable and I was suffused with shame and despair at my own viciousness. Everything vanished; I was alone with a two-year-old girl and many-spired Prague—alone in the midst of night.

II

I was awakened by a pungent stink of blood. I opened my eyes sharply since I thought that it was my own. The very same room embraced me as it had before. And yet it was not quite the same. The sleeping bag beside me was empty. I realized that Tomas had been gone for a considerable time. I was assailed by the nostalgia of a person left abandoned and deserted. In the kitchen (I knew it was there) something had happened, something I had lost in my sleep. Something they let me lose. I also knew that they were all in there.

My eyes wandered over the distant ceiling and I didn't know whether I ought to go in there. I tossed from side to side in my sleeping bag. Meanwhile the precious seconds of some unknown event were running on without me. The door to the kitchen was closed and a light shone under it. Indistinct noises were to be heard but they were nothing to do with me. It was a matter of complete indifference to them that I was here, that I had awakened and was listening to them. I could not smell blood. It was absurd that I had been awakened by the smell of blood. I had no idea how blood smelled.

I got up with a sharp motion. I didn't want to be here for another moment. The room was now a repulsive and collapsed solitude and I could not wait to be with my own kind.

In the kitchen they were all standing in a circle. Andrei

lay on the sofa and Tomas was bending over him. I could not easily see over his back and so I bent over to one side and glimpsed Andrei's naked arm, half-covered in dried blood. It was torn by a long wound from shoulder to elbow. Tomas was cleaning around it with a lace handkerchief that he was wetting in a small bowl of water. Without a word I joined the others.

Tomas now once again squared his shoulders and dipped the handkerchief in the water. Andrei had an air of boredom, but exhaustion and rebellion were reflected in his unbelievably dark eyes. Tomas did not caress the wound. Bit by bit he wiped away the blood and where he could not, he scrubbed forcefully. In those moments I felt as if he were scrubbing at my innards. Simeonu, Mirela, and Livie gazed reverently beneath his hands. Livie squeezed Andrei's uninjured arm between her palms, more from responsibility than from pity. As if everyone knew that for Andrei this was only a short rest on his journey. They did not deny him this or try to appropriate it. I remembered the journey from the station. Then, Andrei had shielded both women with his body. He had denied them nothing.

The boiling water began to whistle. Tomas grasped the needle and threaded it. Nobody asked whether it had to be this way. Either they had discussed it earlier or their reverence for him precluded any questions. These moments were his alone. I felt ashamed that my suspicions of him had been so base.

He dipped the needle and thread into the bubbling water. "Under these conditions it scarcely matters," he remarked apologetically. A few incomprehensible words were passed. "Leave us alone," I think Andrei said.

Simeonu turned away. Finally he noticed that I was present and after him so did the others—it really looked as though they had forgotten about me.

I went back to the room to get dressed. The inextinguishable cold squatted in every corner. When I returned yellow specks were swirling around the kitchen and arranging themselves in double ranks. I asked how Andrei had come to be hurt. They said little and that unwillingly.

Andrei had been at a meeting of some society. Just before midnight the police had broken into the house. Andrei had jumped out of a window and escaped across an unlit yard. It was then that he had torn his arm on some spike. It seemed to be out of the question for him to go to a doctor.

Andrei does not know how many of his friends were caught. Or he doesn't want to say. He doesn't even know if the police know about him. In the morning he will leave home and come back when his arm has healed.

"Where were you actually going when we met you at the station?"

"To my sister's, in the foothills."

I am digressing foolishly, I thought to myself. But Simeonu went on regardless. About his sister and her farm, and the countryside there in the foothills. About the road between the trees. I was only half listening. Why should I be interested at this time of night?

"And Andrei? Was he supposed to be going with you?"

"No."

The yellow spots flowed into one large spot. Andrei and his fate lay here like alien structures, or bodies fallen from another story in the house. They could neither be incorporated nor thrown back. The best thing would be to cover them with a blanket and pretend that they were not there. Or just to leave them and go away.

Livie was shaking inside her coat like an aspen leaf. "Go and lie down," said the father in their own language. "It is no longer necessary for you to be here." Mirela gazed into space with dumb resignation: If this man, lying here, had once been the boy she had taken by the hand for walks, then what was there in the world that could not happen?

Alien and brave, Andrei was lying in front of us. All this because he had remained himself. Much too much himself.

His love and theirs could find no point of intersection. I felt terribly sorry, but for myself, not for Andrei. After all, how different had my own fate been? How different would my own return from this Country be, if I were to be wounded myself? I could end up exactly as he had. I saw before my eyes an alien version of myself.

"You were brilliant," I told Tomas before we fell asleep.

"But not everyone has to know how to deal with sick people," I said to myself inside.

III

Just before I fell asleep, strange thoughts once again wandered around in my head. First I was carried back to the express as it glided over the first few meters of the Country. No-man's-land, surrounded by barbed wire . . . and Romu by the toilet. Remu, smiling in the compartment. The hours that had trickled away since then gaped before it and myself, like a terrifying chasm in the jaws of which everything vanished.

Dreams began to parade in front of me, unrelated to space and time. Hardly had one of them left than another appeared on the screen, and I had no way of controlling which it would be. Landscapes, people, feelings. Sometimes ingenious constructions, at other times only traces of a meaning that remained hidden. Unclaimed messages.

Then I was lying on a bed in my parents' flat. I was injured, and could not move from my place. Somebody was calling me to come in to dinner. It was impossible. My parents' faces loomed over me like obituaries.

In the background—behind the bookcase, the candlestick, the ceiling; behind the window that looked onto the street—shone the star of the coming day. The journey was inscribed on it, and the first steps of the journey had already been taken.

In the morning I took care to wake early. I certainly succeeded: while Tomas still slept, I wandered to and fro across the room. It was only half past five. Outside, a banal December day had awakened itself, with nothing in common with a feast of rebirth. The wheels of the machine were not yet turning and I saw no reason why I should crank them out of immobility. It seemed to me that everything that I had looked forward to in life and that had had some meaning had already happened long before.

But then one single thought allowed hopelessness to return to its opposite. This was when I realized that there existed in the world a girl whose name was Livie.

"Livie laughs at me and invites me into the new day," I thought and was surprised at the vastness of the difference: with her or without her.

"What touches her has meaning and this dawn has slashed the veins of all the rest."

IV

Andrei was shouting at Livie and Livie was shouting at Andrei, although their voices were muffled behind the kitchen door. Andrei was annoyed because of us—I was sure of it. The hour of my love had struck.

"What do you see in these foreigners? We should deal with our own affairs by ourselves," Andrei was saying, I think.

"Please be quiet! What harm have they done to you?" Livie answered, I think.

The door banged and then another slammed in the hall. In the ensuing silence there were no winners or losers. The air returned to the vacuum. It chimed six.

Livie went back into the kitchen and stayed there. Alone with herself at six o'clock in the morning. My heart was hammering. At the opposite end of the room the door was silent between the tight legs of the wall. She was behind it, embraced by yellow solitude. I was overwhelmed by an uncontrollable terror at the opportunity. I saw the kitchen sink, the tap, the pale blue table. The hour had yielded her up and everything depended only on me. Darkness continued to surround me. I knew that if I was not determined . . .

I opened the door. She was sitting on a chair pulled away from the blue table. Her hair was hanging loose over her shoulders. I closed the door behind me.

"You are here in the first light, all alone?" Her eyes caught mine. They approached as I did. She stood up as if she knew what was coming. Her eyes flashed with forgetfulness. I put my arms around her. Warm lips closed on mine.

I held her in my arms and she was alive. I kissed her thin lips. The knowledge of response multiplied my ardor a thousandfold. We sank to the cooling floor. She was making whimpering, endlessly longing sounds, inviting me to enter. I felt her skin in the folds of her dress. It was hot and there was always more of it. I pressed my mouth to her groin. What I had once thought ugly was now sweet and beautiful. In a mad frenzy I threw myself on her.

She was wiping the semen from her thigh. I held her glistening hips in my hands. She arched her body lasciviously and looked at me with veiled eyes. I realized that she was a citizen of another state, and this unbelievable freedom between us aroused me. When I entered her for the second time she bent her head backward.

For a long time we sat under the table leaning against its wooden legs. The minutes dripped down behind us, spilling on the floor around us. She was sitting in the same position as when I had withdrawn from her. She seemed to me stronger then than at any time before, and I also seemed very strong to myself. I pressed her hand and we stood up slowly. I bruised my back on the tabletop.

We opened the window and sat on the sill. Far below us someone's steps were sounding in the darkness. The warm damp air streamed into the kitchen. The thaw.

"It's really time you left," she said.

I was still holding her hand. I looked at her questioningly.

"If they catch my father with it, they'll shoot him. They may spare you. He would go but he can't because he's got us. I gave him sleeping pills." I shivered.

"And what if I hadn't woken up?"

"That would have been cowardice on your part."

The depth where this touched me was too deep: this slim and sensitive girl was sending me to die for my honor. What weights are being loaded on to the scales now? Love? Duty? Sacrifice? Honor? If they shoot me then she will honor my grave all her life and give herself to no one. She attracted me inexpressibly. She ought to become the religion of my life. The giver of absolution and of law.

"It really is time now," she said tenderly. "Or you won't make it. Remember!"

I walked rapidly and noiselessly to the door. "And what exactly?"

She handed me several folded papers. "Father transcribed everything. You know anyway." She smiled. Her long brown hair made a shadow on her face.

I put on my coat and hung the case with the documents in it around my neck.

"Here is a map to help you find my uncle. The seventh street to the left, eleventh to the right, fourth entrance on the right, fourth floor. Augusto Cudean. By seven-thirty."

I stared mutely at the map she had so carefully prepared. How long had she known that it would end the way it was ending?

I walked into the morning corridor above the unlit stairs. Livie's eyes were full of godless love. Now I already knew her smooth buttocks.

Mist. Without hesitating I started off northward; the sound of my footsteps piled up to make invisible walls. The ice was thawing slightly and it stuck to my soles.

I crossed to the other side and counted the side streets:

one, two. . . . The street was beginning to fill up with pedestrians. But each one of them was as solitary as I. Expectation reigned, hot as her groin. Except that this morning the heart of revolt did not start beating, the bells tolled no alarm, and time dragged on, chained to the old treadmill. Heavy warm clouds enveloped the city. People were setting out on a journey with festive dedication in their souls. But then, arriving at work, they saw the faces of the others emerging from milky solitude and realized that they had nothing to tell them. What they wanted could not be expressed. Wordlessly, they turned to their machines.

I was counting the side streets and Livie was stuck inside me. I could still feel particles of her body on my skin. Again and again I recalled her face. She had not considered it necessary to give me the slightest explanation. The absolute incredibleness of her actions toward me spoke of an unlimited trust in my understanding. A trust so great and heavy that at one moment I staggered underneath it and at another it held me up. In these latter moments we faced each other standing erect. We did not touch each other; it was only that the proud nipples of her small breasts were reaching out toward my chest. A chill ran through me.

I still couldn't come to terms with the fact that she was the same girl I had met at the station. At that time she had had a suitcase and a fur coat and she had looked like a flower, protected in the midst of her family. She had attracted me from the beginning. But I wouldn't have expected it of her. It was always unthinkably far from the first surreptitious glance to naked sweaty passion.

At street corners I passed armed guards and although I nearly bumped into them in this misty environment they left me alone. I slipped up to the house in which Augusto Cudean was supposed to live. In front of me there were huge heavy doors of peeling wood and I was gripped by anxiety as it struck me that I might never see those dear to me again. It was a quarter to eight. The space around me was becoming lighter but there was no one close enough to see me entering. I felt as if I had been launched in a rocket that was forever heading toward unlimited distances of loneliness. Down on Earth, Livie had already returned from the launch pad into life. She has hung a bunch of roses on the wall.

On the fourth floor I pushed the bell with the name Augusto Cudean. Nothing stirred. I heard Livie's words: "They may spare you." The house was incomparably poorer than the one I had known. Wires and single bricks were protruding from the walls. The paint was peeling off in great flakes. I rang once again on the warped, corroded door. Steps sounded below, and headed upward. The light went out and came on again. On the stairs a dog started barking. It was the high-pitched hysterical bark of a lapdog. I wasn't going to wait any longer and I started to run quickly down the stairs. At the second floor I passed an obese lady with a little dog. "What could she have got so fat on?" I wondered.

I looked around. The house was really not under surveillance. I realized that under my jacket I was carrying the erupted conscience of Professor Cudean. And this in turn could become the erupted conscience of the people of this city. And now it was up to me whether it would speak out. Livie had made love with me on the floor. On the cold floor under the eyes of the yellow walls and pale blue table.

I returned upstairs and with helpless stubbornness rang and rang. Behind the door the dog started to bark. Then something rustled, and the fat lady opened the door. "Augusto Cudean? " I asked. She mumbled something unintelligible. She emitted it directly from her throat, and her bloated cheeks almost failed to move. "Sprechen Sie Deutsch?" I asked. The dog was attacking my legs. She stared at me like a calf with unmoving and wide-open eyes. I took the papers out and handed them to her folded. "Simeonu. Simeonu Cudean." She glanced over the papers and seemed to be reading. She turned several pages over. Uncomprehendingly she shook her head and handed them back to me. She shrugged and said something again. "Where's Augusto? Augusto!" I tried to break through the barrier. Finally her unusually open eyes lit up and she limped into the bowels of the flat. She was wearing stockings through which her grandmotherly legs could be seen. The dog ran after her with an appreciative whiffling.

"Maybe something after all," I thought. The fat lady was already rushing back. In her hand she was holding some papers, which she gave me joyfully. I looked at the papers. They were blank. "Ehaa," she hooted at me. I looked at her with desperation. Happy at our understanding she was smiling from ear to ear. I smiled too. "Thank you. Thank you very much. Multsumesc."

The smile exhausted me completely. I shot out of the house wanting to vomit and laugh despairingly. At this moment a tiny whipping-boy appeared in front of me. I kicked him in the stomach with all my strength. He folded to the ground like a burst ball. A terrible stench issued from the crack. I grabbed the boy by the hair and dragged him after me. The stench followed us. The ice stuck more than ever. In a while a fence and a garden appeared on the right. I swung the deflated body and threw it over the fence into the still-undefiled snow. I walked further down the paling street. The conscience of Professor Cudean was gushing from the folded papers into my trousers.

All of a sudden I realized that I knew the street. While on the left there were still apartment houses, on the right a double row of barbed wire unwound itself along the top of a wooden barrier. Toward the country of production halls, warehouses, factory walls. Thinning crowds of workers cut the mist into long thin rags. I let them lead me as if I were one of them. The smooth trunks of trees ran backward.

At the edge of the road a heavy armed vehicle now emerged. "It is nearly impossible to deliver the demands to the appointed place," my skeptical "I" commented. "Not because someone will prevent you, but because you don't know where. How many factories do you think this town has? In how many corners of this extruded morning mist is there a march like this going on? She said by seven-thirty. She has given you the wrong information."

I trod silently on.

"She couldn't have known any more," I breathed. I somehow felt that none of this could have happened otherwise. And cannot. And I even wanted it like this. The moisture had already penetrated my clothes and spread a strange chill there. I plodded on resignedly with the others.

"Look at that boy, for example," my skeptical "I" continued. "He is scarcely more than a boy, is he? Now his cap has slid down over his forehead. That's because it's so big. What do you think the revised demands will mean to him? You'd do better to give him bread and salami."

"I have no bread," I said. "And I haven't had breakfast yet."

As I walked and walked it occurred to me that I could take Livie home with me. Home to Prague and live with her there. But I realized that in that case I would have lost everything. All of Livie in herself. Like a Medusa pulled onto dry ground. Maybe she would want a washing machine, a refrigerator, a television. She could stuff herself with cream cakes from morning to night. Until she was unimaginably fat. Or else she would worry herself to death.

The stream of people was turning into a gate. Again an armored vehicle. The way to the factory led between the porter and the black and white bar. The mist, a red slogan, and a five-pointed star. Behind the gate two officers were conducting body searches. The porter was smiling bitterly. He was a giant of a man with an unshaven face. It was as if Remu was looking at me through this man's eyes. I realized that he was my only chance. "Augusto Cudean?" I asked quietly. He thought for a while. "Nu." He towered over me, exuding fellow feeling. His quilted trousers and coat made him still larger. I handed the professor's demands to him. There was no point in taking them any further.

The porter held the papers up to his chestnut-brown eyes. Suddenly he came to life, and looked at me with surprise. At the same moment one of the officers doing the body searches noticed us. There was nothing to be done. The officer set out haughtily toward us.

He snatched the papers from the porter's hanging hand, uttering throaty and unintelligible threats that the huge unshaven porter accepted like a lamb. The officer stepped to one side and without even looking at the sheets of paper started to tear them into tiny pieces. "I can tear it up whatever it is," he meant to tell us. The shreds fell under his feet onto the furrowed ground.

The fact that this sad event was so very fortunate for us filled us with a shameful melancholy. Yes, it meant that we would escape with our skins. And it also meant that the demands with which the workers would embark on the strike would not now be changed by anybody. The porter and I remained standing by the bar without moving; the officer returned with dignity to his undignified work and took no further notice of us. We gave each other a long look. No, it hadn't worked. We preferred to look upward, and at that moment we could both have sworn that among the impenetrable layers of mist we could see great wings stretching over us. I started to run.

v

Toward noon dissatisfaction began to grow in the workplaces. Those who had originally believed that the holiday mood did not create the right conditions for action and who therefore wanted to delay their declaration until reports of the gathering discontent were coming in from all over the Country, were finally proved wrong. What people had experienced over the last few days had been the most terrible mirror of wretchedness ever to enter their homes. Misery at Christmas was a quiet whip, but a strong one. It lashed unceasingly and lashed everyone. It whipped mothers and children alike. It whipped fathers in the midst of their families. And so, despite the soldiers' threats, small groups collected in production halls. The groups joined up into crowds. At a quarter past twelve the lone wail of a siren was the only sound to float above the northwestern outskirts of the city. Half an hour later not one of the larger factories was working.

I went through the mist against the weakening current of the morning shift. Something set me jumping frivolously. Nevertheless: the papers torn up, soaked, the content lost, the mission come to nothing. The happiness that had taken hold of me against all logic allowed me to breathe deeply and joyously. The fact that I did not have to go to work anywhere was warming. "Conscience requires no victory," I said to myself. "Conscience will prevail again, just because it has once existed."

"Conscience will prevail again, just because it has once existed." I repeated the insistent phrase. In a few places holes were appearing in the crust of ice. They were strewn around the area just like the shreds of demands tossed away by the officer. I stopped. I felt no reproaches but a peculiar knowledge that unrealized possibilities are no less significant than those that finally enter the stream of events. "So you see, Livie, so you see, Professor, so you see, Mr. Factory Porter. We have a shared secret. It is about something that was not, but could have been."

The chestnut eyes of the porter. Eyes aiming into legend and bearing witness. Yes, perhaps they will not keep silence about the strange foreigner with the inscribed papers in his hand. They will give a report about the content of those papers, at least the few lines that they caught and their untimely destruction. Perhaps this part of their testimony will give rise to stories of a secret force offering services to the rising at one of the factory forecourts. Perhaps this story will then nourish new hope and a new rising. Perhaps . . .

Silence slapped me in the face. Disbelievingly I looked around me. The space around me had become lighter and the white veil of mist would scatter at any moment. Over the rooftops dark clouds had formed. The street, not yet quite clear but now visible to its end, reflected an unusual calm. I stretched my ears, but nothing came, even from the distance, that I could call the voice of a strike. At that moment I was seized by an unreasoning suspicion that ultimately I was the person responsible for this. It seemed that even the soldiers at the opposite corner had been thrown off balance. They shifted from foot to foot and pointed their loaded submachine guns at me out of boredom. I stepped out. On the left there appeared the house where Augusto Cudean was supposed to live. I turned my head away.

Circles started to form before my eyes and everything looked as if wrapped in a gelatinous membrane. I walked on faster; Livie was lost somewhere out of sight and an unwonted weakness carried me down through the withdrawing street. The shops remained closed and the space around them empty. Only in front of a closed bakery was a lengthy line forming. I could see nothing more than indistinct local faces there. Despite what were strange circumstances for me the town was already less surprising and less foreign. The hobbling old man who nodded at me from the line certainly wanted nothing more than a cigarette. I had none and I was less interested in him than in the strike that had still to break out. Again and again I strained for sounds coming from the distance. Nothing. The dripping of water from roofs.

At last the familiar house. Identification number 1023 (the same number as the house of my childhood). Here however instead of bells only wires were sticking out from the wall. They drew my attention as if from a long way off. I could not imagine what to say to Livie with other people present. The kitchen had yellow walls and we had burned in it before the day had even started. But what now?

It was cold in the house and possibly even darker than before. There was a roaring in my ears. From the open cellar came the rustling of something living. It struck me that it might be Livie. The image of her buttocks came back to me arousingly close. Unthinkingly I set off after the sound.

First I entered a short dark corridor that after perhaps two meters turned sharply to the right. From behind the corner emanated a reddish glow. A hardly perceptible current of cellar air brushed by me. I stopped at the threshold of an unexpectedly large room on the other side of which a gang of workmen were digging in loose gray attire. They had dug under the whole of one wall and it was hanging over empty space. They were now digging under another wall. In the middle of the room a gray cat was sitting over the carcass of a dove and there was blood on its face. When it noticed me, it raised its head and gave me a long assessing look with its green eyes. It seemed to me that the dove moved imperceptibly. The cat was the only creature in the room to have noticed me despite the fact that my arrival had not been noiseless. The indifference of the workmen provoked me. "'Scuse me . . . " I moved forward into the room. The cat seized the dove and dragged it away. "'Scuse me . . ." But the workmen went on minding their own business. It seemed to me that there were five of them but my state of mind prevented me from seeing them individually. I stood somewhere between them; I could have touched the nearest one. Again and again he raised his gray arms; the pickax descended on the wall; dust swirled and there was a sprinkling of red sand. It is possible that the room was echoing with rumbling blows. "'Scuse me . . . "

I was beginning to realize that I couldn't expect any response and this knowledge filled me with dejection and fear. It was an unbounded fear for all those who were dear to me. "Livie." (Only then did I remember that I had been looking for her there.) I backed slowly to the door. From one side came the sound of contented feline munching.

She sat unmoving and slim on the topmost stair. We looked at each other for a long time without moving. We enjoyed what we did not have to say. It had not happened to either of us in our lives before. She was a young girl. I ran up the last few steps and hid her under my body. I wanted to cover her up completely: I squeezed her from as many sides as possible and whispered into her pointed ears in Czech: "I won't give you up, my little girl; not to anybody in the world, not to anybody."

VI

She stopped in the narrow attic entrance. "Wait for me here," she said, "I have to tell my parents that you have returned." She then looked at me devotedly: "They reproached me; they said that I would have you on my conscience. But it was your free decision . . . wasn't it?" Devotion changed to pleading.

"You know best how it was," I said.

"So you are angry with me?"

"Let's not talk about it."

After these last words she bent her head and started to leave. "Livie," I whispered. She turned round. "But I didn't deliver the demands. Augusto was not at home." She was at my side in an instant. She attached herself to me like a nymph. I put my hands on her shoulders and squeezed. She sighed. "She is so distinct a character," I thought.

She softly disentangled herself from my grasp and ran downstairs. "Livie," I whispered once more. She was already holding the key and I could see how deeply she was embedded in all this around her. "What will you tell your parents about where you are going?"

"Where would I want to go? I'm going for a walk. Tomas

has gone for a walk as well," she said. The door slammed behind her.

I slowly shifted myself under a large wooden beam. My nausea eased and I could distinguish clear forms around me. The news that Tomas had gone for a walk wandered around in my head. Somehow I had stopped believing that he would do this kind of thing. I realized that I was actually betraying him by my relationship with Livie. I would definitely not like to be in his position.

Water was dripping on the dust-covered floor from a gap between the tiles. The distant dormer window shed a little light here and a pile of debris emerged from the half-light behind the chimney shaft. A few rags lay on the blackened beam. So this was the world of her childhood. Here she had played with the cat and helped her mother to hang the laundry. Without any fear of the future in her small girl's soul. I could feel her everywhere here. But the walls that mutely culminated here led all the way to the bottom—to the foundations. An evil foreboding touched me. The rising wind struck at the roof.

I pushed up the dormer window and looked out. Perceptibly warmer air brushed my face. The lowest layer of cloud had broken up and the remaining shreds were caught on the slopes of forested hills. The woods darkened and the cloud cover, still low, remained hanging over the city of which I could see only the opposite house. Lumps of ice were shriveling unpleasantly and slipped down the tiles to the guttering.

At last she was standing beside me. In her hand she held a lump of yellow mash.

"It's the saddest thing," she said thoughtfully. "When there is a thaw but spring is still far away." She gave me the lump and pronounced its unknown name. I was surprised at how compact and dry it was. Something between a paste and a pancake. I bit into it; the bland taste melted on my tongue and slowly ran down into my stomach. Nothing special but it was edible. It even whispered to me in confidence that it would nourish me, which slightly took me aback. As well as the evident devotion in Livie's eyes, which made me belong with her more than at any time before.

"In a little while I have to take mother's place in the line," she said.

Unthinkingly I stared at her and at the mushroom balls of cloud.

"You look somehow serious." She looked at me with concern.

For a moment I longed to tell her what I had seen in the cellar of her house. But I saw that I couldn't and this meant that I was already really losing her. I pressed her to myself; her head on my shoulder. "It's just your imagination," I whispered placatingly. Desire started to take hold of me. She was still unbelievably new in my life and for that reason arousing. If someone had been looking from the uppermost windows of the house opposite they would have seen our heads in the dormer window.

Oh yes, our two heads in the dormer window. The soaked banners of the hills pointed at the streets that were invisible to us; church spires and factory chimneys stood immobile behind them. It was as if we had stepped out of the riverbed of time that was underneath us and around us. "Do you remember," I said, "how we stood above your city full of dirt and poverty and the ramparts of the woods challenged us to call up an echo that the wind blew away? That was one of our last moments before the course of time wore us away." She smiled painfully; and then everything happened at breakneck speed. "We shall die when one of us dies."

The brakes screamed and the door opened.

"What does your father say about the fact that nothing's happening?" I asked.

Somewhere under our line of vision heavy boots hit the pavement. It was probably several pairs and it was difficult to guess which house they were making for. Nevertheless, cold gripped me and I had the feeling that someone was crawling up my trouser-legs as I stood leaning my chest against the window ledge. The steps then died away and a clearly recognizable whiff of house air sailed past us.

Somebody was now quite definitely crawling up my trousers. I braced myself on my arms and pulled my upper body toward the guttering. The wooden edge dug into my stomach and the uneaten paste stuck between the fingers of one hand. I still managed to notice that Livie was clutching tightly onto my jacket.

Finally I got my head above the gutter and saw a stationary limousine. It was as if patches of thawing ice were splintering against its metal burnish; blood rushed to my head, I was left only a few last moments of certainty that I would be able to pull myself back. A man was stamping beside the limousine and this time there could be no doubt who it was: It was Romu.

"They're probably coming somewhere here," I told Livie breathlessly, back in safety once more.

"They?" she asked darkly.

"Is there any way through to another entrance?" I continued, instead of giving the answer that she knew anyway.

"Yes," she said. "But I'm not running away from here. And anyway I have nowhere to run."

During our conversation the steps were coming nearer and now they disappeared on the last floor. As quietly as possible we moved toward the exit. As we held hands bits of the paste glued us together. From the corridor we could hear individual words. Then the bell started to ring and someone's hand beat on the door.

We got to a place where a square trap door allowed us to squat down and follow all the events taking place. I would have been happier if there had been no such place.

Simeonu opened the door and those entering (there must have been two) shoved him into the corridor. I grabbed

Livie around the chest and shoulders. She started but I held her as if in a vise. There was a lot of screaming; I caught the word "Andrei." Simeonu shrugged his shoulders. One of the arrivals slapped his face and at the sharp sound Livie dug her head into my jacket. All heroism dissolved and the professor's swelling face was now turned toward us. I felt faint and nauseated. I could see the face of the goon closest to me and it resembled the face from the Europa restaurant. Only perhaps it was even more anonymous. The figure of Romu, waiting outside, passed through my mind.

More blows rained on the terrified professor. All the commandments turned inside out, my innards churned inside me. Now they had grasped the professor around the shoulders and were giving him friendly slaps. Thwack!! Another blow. I didn't want to see it but I had to. Thwack!! I wanted to scream "shame." But on my own behalf. It shamed me to see him this way. Him—the aging father of a family, a teacher, an honored citizen, humiliated at the door of his own flat. Wretched Simeonu. Now he inspired no glimmer of reverence; blood was gushing from the corner of his mouth and face to face with possible death he shook with fear. Livie trembled in my embrace.

But death did not come. Instead the visitors dusted themselves off as if the whole thing had been incidental and gave a routine smile—the local variant of that vulgar vacuity that gives them away on all the street corners of the world. The one nearer to me could have been about forty. He stood so near that I could even see the tufts of hair peeking out from his nose. His skin showed the ingrained dirt of the terrain— a dirt that defied all washing and stinks even if scented.

They forced their way, which lay naked before them in dumb astonishment. Simeonu hesitated. If I had wanted I could have given him a signal, but what could I have communicated? He was already following them resignedly. From inside came the sounds of a house-search. "What about our sleeping bags?" I whispered. "I put them away," she breathed and dug her fingers so hard into my arm that I jumped.

It didn't take longer than two minutes and the policemen reappeared. They were suddenly in a hurry. They bowed to Simeonu and shook his hand. "Good-bye, Professor," "Keep well, Professor." Although they had not found Andrei I got the impression that they were leaving thoroughly satisfied. They must have known in advance that he was not there.

The professor stood solitary in the doorway; he resembled a plucked bird. His longish thinning hair stuck out in all directions and blood, which he had not wiped off, had dried on his chin. An abandoned plucked bird. He fingered the wound. Above him a worn-out lavatory chain appeared. He raised his hand, grabbed the chain, and pulled. The sluice-gates rumbled and the door banged. Just before it happened I caught myself saying, against my will, "Just vanish! Get out of our sight."

Livie started sobbing in my grasp. She uttered something unintelligible. All at one she tried to get up, but I prevented her. She raised her head to me in surprise. her face convulsed, unpleasantly contorted. "We have to go to him," she said.

"You want to go after him?"

"He is my father after all. He needs us."

"What he most needs now is himself. Only himself," I said. "He definitely doesn't need his children." I tried to pour calm into her from my open palms. In fact I was not holding her any more.

"But he is my father," she said desperately. She said it so convincingly that I hesitated. What if ultimately she was right and I was dragging idiotic honor into it? Women have a different understanding—merciful women. I felt it physically impossible to go after him. My whole organism felt it. "If I were in his place," I told myself, "I would want to be alone."

Immediately I had said this to myself, I realized that it was not true. I would have wanted to be with her. Her closeness would be what I would have sought. I would have laid my head in her hands. I would have accepted absolution from her. The Absolution that only a woman can give.

"Let's get some fresh air by the window."

She got up like a poorly functioning machine. My legs were also folding under me. After a few steps things sorted themselves out in my head. "Livie, if you want, perhaps you should go to him." She looked at me absently, in confusion. "You should go to him," I repeated. "Don't tell him that we saw it all. Tell him that we just came in. Tell him that I'll come in a moment."

She faced me uncertainly, deserted. All her will had drained away somewhere. "Martin, . . . but come with me at least to the door," she breathed at last.

"Actually," I stepped down into the corridor myself, "I wanted to show you one man. He was standing by their car a while ago. We met him in the train. From then on it's as if he's been following us. A certain Romu."

She shrugged her shoulders. It was apparent that just now she wasn't interested.

I wandered through the attic again. By now the car had certainly left. Romu had disappeared and with him any hope that I might grasp something. Thoughts were running around in my head half in Czech and half in German. Nothing, absolutely nothing was left in my hands. When I had talked to the professor or to Livie it had been different. Every word had been like a small gift.

The wind spun in the unreachable corners of the attic. To kill time I paced from place to place. I wanted something important but I could not express what. I looked at my watch. It was only eleven. It was unbelievable how long the day lasted here. Outside it was beginning to look like rain. Spring. I wished that spring would come.

Soon I realized that there was no sense in playing this stupid game. Simeonu was a self-sufficient man who aroused my respect. If he needed my charity, the respect would have disappeared. "Everyone needs charity," said my skeptical "I." "You are living on credit if you don't want to give it." In the meantime I rang the bell and frightened whispering could be heard from inside. It occurred to me that, unfortunately, to be a policeman might be quite amusing.

The professor opened the door and I immediately realized that he knew everything. I stood there in embarrassment. He gave a self-deprecating smile. "You will have to get used to this kind of thing here. We've had to get used to it."

"Are you telling me," I stuttered confusedly, "that this has happened to you before?"

"Several times," he said calmly. "Once even at the blackboard. In front of my class."

I did not understand. I could vividly remember the desperate expression on his face when the blows were falling. Even the wretched way that he had frozen at his doorway— entirely alone, alone with his humiliation. No more than fifteen minutes had gone by since then. And he . . . Livie was leaning on the doorframe. "Father thought that they had broken a tooth. But it wasn't a real one." She laughed. I realized that I was only a stupid Central European.

Mirela and Tomas came in a moment after me. "We've only got two loaves," he reported from the door. "They wouldn't give us any more. They said that there must be enough to go round. But even so there won't be."

A relaxed mood entered with Tomas. "It's time for a regular meal," he called in Czech. I turned to them: "We are inviting you to a proper lunch." And then I pulled out a whole salami. Tomas dug out a tin and a loaf of bread. I added a tube of butter spread, a hunk of smoked cheese and a box of vitamin drink. Tomas fished out the forgotten schnitzels, powdered custard, and a bar of chocolate. We gathered it all together and took it into the kitchen. Mirela blocked our way and Simeonu despairingly tugged my sleeve. Somehow they were offended. But we stood our ground. I asked Simeonu to bring a bottle of home liquor—that would be their contribution. He calmed down: he even persuaded Mirela, who looked pugnacious, to leave the kitchen. After a moment she returned and to embarrassment on both sides showed us where she kept the plates and cutlery. I felt like a creditor looking over the flat and all its effects.

Among the crockery a few interesting pieces were stored haphazardly. One teapot looked Chinese. The cups were dreadful. Green-blue crockery shone optimistically.

Livie came and fleetingly pressed my palm. Tomas gave an ironical half-smile. "I see you haven't been idle," he said in Czech.

I was glad that he knew about us—it gave a pleasant feeling of ownership. And he did not even seem disappointed. To him it had only been a game.

While we hovered around the stove silence resounded more and more perceptibly from the other room. I heard it first by chance and then it slid through the open doors in the form of a thick snake exploring the terrain with its forked tongue. The snake stopped at my foot and the jagged line along its back was disappearing behind the door corner. Both parents were certainly there—they had to be there—and their silence was aimed at me. Perhaps we were depriving them of more than all the secret policemen in the world could take.

"Look, do you know what's bothering them?" said Tomas suddenly.

"No, I don't." I put down a plate and went to the parents with empty hands. They were sitting helplessly sunken in their chairs. In front of them stood three unmarked bottles but their gaze was fixed elsewhere. I smiled and Simeonu tried to smile too. I felt my face stretch in a broad gourmet's smile. It was stronger than me, and through me it infected them. "Your good health!" said Simeonu almost slavonically and he grasped one of the bottles. "Your health."

We sat down to the laden table. Simeonu sniffed at the butter with curiosity. "Is this usual in your country?" "It's usual."

"Wait!" commanded Tomas suddenly. "What's that!?" We fell silent and through the window the oscillating wail of a siren beat a path to us. Weakened by distance it presented itself to us unobtrusively, almost inaudibly. Simeonu uttered an animal cry and hurled himself at the window. He dragged Mirela in his wake and Livie ran after them. They embraced each other stormily while I and Tomas had only just risen from our chairs. They opened the shutters and the sound became more distinct. A window opened in the house opposite. Behind it stood a woman with a scarf on her head and they called out to her in friendly tones. The woman replied in a yodeling voice.

Tomas and I, returned to each other, stood behind them all. The warm air was seeping from the outside and circling us. The woman opposite took off her headscarf and threw it into the street. The scarf slowly fell to the ground.

"Tomas . . . it's hard for me to remember what was yesterday and what I was living for this morning," I said. "The day before yesterday is entirely lost to me. It's been so long since Christmas."

VII

From the sky, which was unnaturally near, smooth shapes resembling stalactites hung above our heads. Others reached down to waist level and some almost to the stony ground. They all broadened out into the heights like solitary female legs.

Livie and I were walking in a narrow, insufficiently light-ed world, and looking for my body. A few other families were also searching here for their fallen. Around us the last remnants of snow thawed to dimly glittering pools. Their surfaces merged into a broad expanse of lake through which we were forced to walk. The water chilled us.

We reached the gates of a football stadium. The porter on duty was idling at the threshold. Livie asked him something—it seemed to me that I heard my name. The guard shook his head and stood back on his heels obstructively. He was old and his stance was weak and ridiculous. "Now what?" I thought. "We don't need to be in this precise place." I didn't understand why Livie was making for this place at all. But she pulled a carton of cigarettes out of her bag and handed it over to the guard so automatically that it took me aback. He was probably expecting this because he opened a creased notebook and started to look something up in it. Suddenly he looked up with surprise: "Czechoslovak!?" Livie nodded obediently. "Dollar!" he commanded and stretched out his hand. Livie pulled out more cigarettes. The guard accepted them but held out his hand again: "Dollar!" he repeated. Livie shook her head.

"Nu Dollar?!"

"Nu."

The guard looked very discontented. He snapped the notebook shut and then opened it again. A long silence followed during which I could hear his rasping breath. I was afraid that he might collapse at any moment.

"Cigarette?" he asked finally. Livie handed him the whole bag. He looked inside and reluctantly hung it on her shoulder. It was clear that this was not a good day for him.

We entered the stadium area curtained with stalactites. I felt that we were nearing our goal. I just didn't know what sort of goal it was supposed to be.

My body was lying alone under an especially broad stalactite. Grief at its undeserved loneliness overwhelmed me. Livie bent down over me. I wanted to take her hand or get closer to her in some other way. But I didn't even try—I had not found out if it was possible. I had an extremely distinct desire to sit in a patisserie in a Prague suburb.

I woke up with a bitter feeling of guilt. The dusk of a December day was already descending on the bedroom. I must have slept for at least an hour. I pushed my head a little way out of the pleasant warmth of the sleeping bag. Livie's parents' marital bed protruded beside me and its obese headboards seemed to warn against excessive passion. I tried to get clear what had happened before I had fallen asleep: We had cleaned up the remnants of the feast. . . . Two had struck and then half past two. A column of army cars had gone by. There had been no news.

I slid back to earth. The stalactites hung and did not hang in the darkening space. I wondered what else this day, started so prematurely, would bring me. On the other side of the room Tomas was contentedly drawing breath. My feeling of guilt now had a discernible origin: to sleep in the daytime was a sin.

"Tomas!" I pulled myself up.

No answer.

"Any news?" He spoke suddenly, as if he had not been asleep.

"No, but it's four o'clock. We ought to get up."

He stretched. "What about that strike of theirs?"

The words "that" and "of theirs" bothered me. I was silent.

"So you see nothing will change." He spoke almost triumphantly. "Did you think they could force something through against the army?"

"Why shouldn't they? Maybe they will."

I preferred to go and wash. Once in the hallway I heard water running in the bathroom. A workman in overalls was bending over the washbasin. His loose trousers were covered with red dust. Now he reached for a towel and wiped his face on it. I waited for him to finish. At last he turned the tap off and walked around me to the hallway. I took his place at the washbasin. After a while the oddity of the whole situation struck me. I ran out of the bathroom. But the workman wasn't there. The hallway rose to the ceiling large and empty. The zinc basin froze with its purposelessness.

I finished my ablutions. On the cold seat—intimately grown into it—I perceived the alien character of everything.

I met other workmen in the kitchen. (I hoped that I would find Livie there.)

This time there were two workmen and the one from the bathroom was not with them. But they were basically identical. With revolting self-assurance they sat on the kitchen sideboard. I had already gone too far to retreat and so I walked right up beside them. "Are the citizens here obliged to make their flat available in this way?" The workmen had nothing to say to me. Only their navels winked at me from under their gray clothes. I was trying to imagine how it looked when they had hard-ons.

I took refuge in the other room. A sound like the gurgling of waterpipes dripped from the tin radio.

An exaggeratedly self-confident voice reproduced an Italian popular song in the local language. If the radio had had remote control someone would long ago have switched it off. But it had only a white on-off button. And so it played on and on. The father, mother, and Livie had obviously been ruminating silently and possibly sleeping for a moment. When I entered Livie fixed me with a deadened stare.

"Your tenants have somehow multiplied," I joked with the underhand idea of resolving what was bothering me. Simeonu and Livie raised their heads as if they had misheard and nobody reacted as if they had understood me. It was exactly what I had feared. "I meant to say," I continued rapidly, "that you are rather intimidated."

An oppressive weighing of words. Simeonu finally realized that this time even his daughter would not come to his aid and he breathed in painfully: "You have come to spend your holidays in our beautiful mountains. To relax after your work. But you have not found what you were looking for in our country. Because our country . . . " Here he faltered: "It is possible that in the end you will be witnesses to something ugly. You have mountains in your own country after all. This is not a good country for you."

I saw how much what he was saying pained him. But despite this I did not understand. My problem was the men in the next room. Livie's deadened eyes were also my problem. I was now unable to look at her as something foreign. She was my Livie and I felt that she didn't belong to me. Everything might be solved if I could embrace her. In these circumstances I could only caress her sharp chin and mouth from afar.

"But we are not sorry that we came here," I said, "so long as it doesn't bother you."

Simeonu gave a small professorial smile that was supposed to show that he understood me but that the obligation to protect us was this time the stronger. "A little while ago," he started, "they broadcast that the workers in our city were called to go back to work immediately. If they don't obey, they will be tried before an extraordinary military court. Apparently the workers have obeyed."

The voice dripping from the radio now assumed a different pitch. The professor had already overcome his original pain and talked like a man who realized what the situation required from him. "We obviously don't know what the real situation is," he continued. "But if you ask for protection at the police station, nothing should happen to you. You are after all citizens of another state. Maybe tomorrow even this won't matter to them." His voice was almost pleading.

Livie stood up and turned her head away. It was already on the tip of my tongue to say "I won't desert your daughter."

"Well," I opened my mouth without knowing what I wanted to say. "It isn't our intention to seek danger on purpose. And we don't want to play any games. But a man must take a decision when life puts him in a particular position. If you understand me, there are moments when whatever used to apply is no longer valid. When whatever you thought or wanted ceases to apply and the only thing valid is what is. We are really not looking for danger. But we can't run away from it when it comes after us itself."

"Father is not throwing you out," blurted Livie. "He means well."

I smiled at her: "I know he is not throwing us out. Or at least that's how I take it. That's why we won't be thrown out."

Simeonu looked offended. "Of course I'm not throwing you out," he said. "But it's not simple for you to stay. You will have to think it over."

"Good. I'll talk about it with Tomas." I looked at Mirela. Although she could not understand us she did not look exactly enthusiastic. I wondered whether Livie resembled her at all. Mirela had coarse graying hair. Her features reflected no special tension. Livie on the other hand was tension incarnate. She definitely took after her father. Mirela was half a head taller than I am.

I had all three in front of me and at my back the kitchen with the workmen about whom only I knew. "If you knew too . . . " I thought. With that I definitely admitted that they didn't know. They knew—they didn't know. With the silence of the workmen there entered into me as well a deep unfathomable silence. So the military tribunal then. I glimpsed the silhouettes of the country cottages to which fathers might never return. How simple destruction is, in the end. I glimpsed the silhouettes of the same houses leveled to the ground. They had leveled them to the ground together with their sheep and their guard-dogs—so that out of the mixture of blood, brick, meat, and beams the grass would grow when there was famine in spring. The sheep brain fell on the dog heart by chance and the dog brain on the sheep heart: the seven-branched candlestick fell on the wooden cross. The sheep will be reeducated as dogs and the dogs as sheep. The families will be moved in between concrete walls.

"So I'll talk about it with Tomas." But I still hadn't gone out. "Livie . . . I would like to ask you about a teapot that you have in the cupboard. Can I show it you?" And when she acquiesced I let her go a pace in front of me so that I could see how she would react to the presence of the workmen. But she did nothing. The kitchen was already empty.

As quietly as possible I embraced her on the opposite side of the door. She kissed me on the lips.

Close up her face was sweetly sharp.

She suddenly cooled. "You will leave in the end anyway," she said in a completely alien voice. It was something for which I hadn't been prepared. Helplessly I pushed her away from me: "What am I supposed to say to that?" She looked at me as if turned to stone. "We will think of something," I said more peaceably. "Or don't you think so?"

Mirela came into the kitchen and so there was no time to get any closer. Irritated and disgusted I went to confer with Tomas.

As if deliberately, Tomas was sitting on the toilet. I walked around the bedroom and every so often turned into the hallway. At last he came out, oddly pale. I explained the situation to him. "I told you it would end this way," he commented. "If it was my aim," I thought, "to ensure that my words came true as often as possible, I would be a skeptic too." Aloud I said, "At least you have a reason to be pleased."

"Me pleased?" he countered. "Not at all. I take no pleasure in other people's misfortunes. And I'm not going home. Even if it isn't safe here."

It was a peculiarity of his that he never experienced anything to the very end, even though he knew about the possibility. We sat on the edge of an unmade white bed. I felt like helplessly retreating under the quilt, as happens to helpless people. "Tomas . . . I have never experienced such perfect understanding with anyone as I have with her." But I was annoyed as soon as I had said it. With each word I was losing something incommunicable.

"Then take her with you," said Tomas simply.

"Take her with me . . . do you think it would be possible?"

"Or leave her here. She doesn't fit anywhere else anyway."

We went back to the room. When Mirela saw Tomas she melted completely and Simeonu rose excitedly. Tomas began to explain to them that we really did not want to leave and I felt that they took it in a completely different way than when I had said it. I sauntered over to the side where Livie was sitting: "Livie . . . life without you would seem empty to me." Only I suddenly didn't know which life I had in mind. The one I had lived up to then? Was it still there? A few vanishing memories, a couple of tins and a couple of connections—was that it? And if not, then maybe some other life, on which I was only now embarking? In this city and in this Country. To let it lead me on? To another country? To the mountains? To destruction?

Livie smiled more bitterly than ever before. But it was clear that my words warmed her. Suddenly she turned to her father: "Father," she said, this time in German. "Martin and I are going upstairs—to look at the city."

Simeonu was so engrossed in his conversation with Tomas that he only nodded absently. We slipped out into the hallway. I could still hear Tomas expounding on healing.

In the hallway I was assailed by fear. It seemed to me that if I went into the bedroom or the kitchen I would meet one of the workmen. In the corridor it could be even worse. Only Livie took me by the hand and her warm touch calmed me.

"Do you like dancing?" she asked in the corridor. Everything was already swimming in impermeable darkness.

"To tell the truth, no. Really not at all"

She fell silent.

We squeezed through the narrow passage to the attic. Under the dormer window the darkness was only a touch lighter. We walked there across the slats. Opposite, weak lamplights illuminated the interiors of model apartments. Today I smelled only the corn mash, pulses, and spirits coming from there. Although it was only half past five the city was already hushed as if sleeping. Nowhere was there the dancing I wanted for her.

I sensed the heavy moist clouds somewhere within reach. The remnants of snow on the tiles were truly the last. In the distance red lights on factory towers whined that nobody wanted to play with them.

"How do you think it will end?" I said. (From what I knew of the people here it was unthinkable that they would all obey the command to a man. And so there was nothing for it but to suppose that somewhere the military tribunal was in session.)

"Nobody knows anything," said Livie. "But Father believes that a lot of people will gather in the morning in front of the largest factory. All their celebrations are held there."

Her words about our leaving continued, even now, to lie heavy on my consciousness. I felt the need to cheer her up somehow, only no words seemed right: "Livie . . . when I finally have to go back home, it definitely won't be forever." I didn't dare to say things that would have had some meaning. The unbounded space of possibility opened up above us. We pulled the glass cover down over the window so as to form a barrier between us and the too distant beauties to which we could not fly or even walk.

"What do you really want from life?" I asked.

"I want it to have value."

We went back to the middle of the attic where we were free of all shapes. She took a few steps away from me and began to undress. She threw the clothes over a wooden strut above her and I threw my clothes over one above me. Finally she stood in front of me wrapped in the hollow darkness.

I sensed the nakedness of her body—her legs, hips, breasts, back; and under my soles I felt cold dust. It seemed to me that the whole universe had here culminated in her.

I approached her in the age-old way. She bent forward. Our simultaneous cry flowed out into the universe.

I held her from behind with open palms over her belly. Then I moved them down to her legs and back to her inner thigh. She bent backward toward me while I stood inside her. Like a fish into water she coalesced into opaque emptiness.

"I would never have believed that such smooth skin was possible," I said. A little cooling sweat already ran down over our bodies. I lifted her up high. There was a smacking sound as I relinquished her. I carried her to the dormer window and back again. We were trembling.

"If someone is conceived by this, I do not envy him," she said.

"Neither do I."

VIII

We dressed and the cold went on shaking us. We crouched down frantically and when this didn't help, we pressed together. Exhausted and chilled through, we sat on the lowest beam. In fact I didn't even feel the real cold; I only knew that I was cold. Our surroundings were lined with invisible cotton wool. I felt like a man who has successfully accomplished all that he is supposed to accomplish.

I involuntarily began to compare the past with the present. And so it happened that I found myself in my apartment—in Prague—among the things to which I was attached. There was my bed, the desk at which I used to sit, and the painting on wood I bought by chance with the crack in the middle.

My life up to now had never seemed banal. But now I felt that it had been. It had been unable to erect anything better than distaste for the public neutralization of body and soul . . . and sometimes not even that. Against the lack of substance only a longing for substance . . . and sometimes not even that. "We are after all the double axis of all stories." The strangely painful words rang in my head without my knowing how they had got there. "Livie," I said, "say that we are not going down yet."

"Not yet." But the cold had completely shattered her voice. Terrified I embraced her. "You are cold!" "No!" I wanted to say something more but instead of comfort that torn-out phrase came into my mind again and I couldn't remember who had uttered it and on what occasion. Moreover it was clear that its peculiar and incomprehensible significance consisted just in this uncertainty. With all the strength of my will I tore myself from reflection and stood up resolutely:

"Come down, or you'll catch cold here! Tomorrow is an important day."

She caught my sleeve like a child.

As tenderly as I could I soothed her: "You know that I would rather stay here too."

Finally she obeyed. We descended the stairs and unlocked the door. In the hallway a weak light already shone. I saw her purple lips and her face exhausted by cold. The moments when she had coalesced with icy emptiness were already gone. Now she was again a creature of sun and spring breezes.

"You should crawl into my sleeping bag," I said. She nodded.

In the bedroom we were surrounded by familiar darkness. I unrolled the sleeping bag and tenderly wrapped her in it up to her ears. Her body was soft and supple—as if devoid of will.

"It's nothing," she whispered.

"I know," I felt her warming up under my hands. I stroked her hair. "Just lie down, my little girl, lie quiet."

"This teapot you were asking about," she started painstakingly, as if she felt some debt: "It belonged to Mother's parents. Mother comes from a Jewish family. The candlestick in the room belonged to them too." "How strange." I wondered, "And your father isn't a Jew?"

"Father? No." She spoke even more softly—I had to bend right down to her lips to understand. "Mother's parents," she continued, "were very rich. They exported furs to Europe."

I remembered the fur coats they had been wearing at the train station. So this was the source of that peculiar air of cultivation, that old-fashioned glow. I pondered for a moment. "You know, when I saw the candlestick in your room I thought that your father was Jewish. He is so educated."

She smiled. "Father is a farmer."

A sleepy contentment settled in the corners of her lips. She had probably told me everything she wanted to say. She looked at me with devoted eyes in which there now resided some unending grief of ages. It resided there without her knowledge.

Tomas came in. "What's going on? Why don't you join us?" The parents came in too.

"No, nothing's going on." I scrambled up from a position that was difficult to explain. "Livie got cold."

Tomas leaned down professionally and touched Livie's forehead and temples: "It isn't by any chance from undernourishment?" Simeonu and Mirela looked at him with unlimited trust. I saw in their eyes how happy it made them to give her to him, if only for healing.

All of a sudden I found myself in the hallway. Nobody had noticed my involuntary exit. "Strange," I thought. "I ought to get on better with the professor than he does."

I went into the kitchen. The workmen were using the opportunity and happily making themselves at home there. Two were sitting pretty behind the table and the third was even stealing glances into the other room. I retreated. Merry voices could be heard from the bedroom but I didn't want to go back. The kitchen was also impossible and the hallway walls closed in on me unmercifully and linked me to the cellar. It seemed to me that I could hear the sound of blows.

The light from the kitchen and hallway fell into the main room. A huge workman was staring indifferently in like a small animal resting in front of its hole. The candlestick recalled Jewishness; hers and mine. "Yes," I realized, "I am Jewish as well. Why did I forget to tell her?"

I marveled at how everything in the room—the furniture, radio, books—lived, as it were, the political situation. The only thing lacking was a map on the table showing the balance of power.

I felt suddenly entirely alone—alone with what was outside. Livie's deep chill had awakened my protective instincts. I opened the door wide. The change that had taken place outside immediately put me on the alert. It was raining. A dense fine drizzle was descending into the streets. The house opposite was vanishing in the falling spray and the gurgling of little streams was audible. The whole world drank and drank.

I stretched out my palm into the space in front of me. It struck me that someone would catch me by the legs and throw me out. My palm became wet and changed in shape. I drew it back—I wanted to look at the transparent miracle that enveloped it. It was water—ordinary water. I wondered what it would change into.

NAKED DAY

I

ANOTHER DINGY MORNING LOOMED UP FROM COURTYARDS and corners and descended on the place where the story was to be played out. From somewhere in the tear-drenched suburbs, still entirely submerged in darkness, several factory lights reached out and trickled down the wet windows in barely perceptible stains. I set out for the toilet but opened the bathroom door by mistake, and Mme. Mirela's white, overhung backside informed me of my error. I slammed the door shut, without quite waking from my half-sleep. "How dry it is—almost like paper," I thought sleepily. Thick morning urine colored the water in the bowl an orange-yellow.

A meaninglessly cruel way to get up. The rain outside stopped: the remaining drops were disappearing from the windows—who knows where. We sat down helplessly on the cold upholstery of the armchairs and nothing gave the impression that some time in the future our stay here would end. The day that had begun with the bare backside of Mme. Mirela could be called nothing other than naked day.

I had still never visited Livie in her own room. I therefore went there now to fulfill the words of Scripture (the Scripture that has not yet been written). It was a small narrow room, scarcely more than a closet. The bulb from the hall was enough to illuminate it. Livie and Andrei had bunk beds, one above the other. Livie was already dressed and lying with her eyes fixed upward. I could have approached her. But it was written: "Thou shalt not come to her bed on the last day."

"Are you ready?" I asked from the door.

She went on lying there, concentrated and her eyes unmoving. Andrei's bed above her had been made up spotlessly.

"Why have we got up so early?"

My sentence stabbed into the emptiness and then vanished like smoke. I realized that for what was to come each must prepare himself alone.

On the way back to the main room I felt a longing for goulash. In my backpack I had a tin of goulash and this reminded me of my position here. Suddenly I wasn't sure if the fact that the events here interested me meant that they also concerned me. What surrounded us was their destiny, their Country. . . . Destiny. In the corridor between room and room I sought my own.

"You take yourself too seriously," said the tapless zinc washbasin. "Stretch out your hand and feel my cool face. Then you will also understand the question that concerns both you and us."

"But, after all, I basically came out of boredom," I said.

"You take yourself too seriously," parroted my skeptical "I."

"I wish I knew whether I could take myself seriously."

Livie came out of her room. I turned to her: "If you don't want us to go to the factory with you then tell me. When what's at stake is so fundamental it's important that everyone should have the same reason for being there . . . that everyone should be equal in having that reason. You have grown up here, you have lived here for more than twenty years. Perhaps you wouldn't be happy if you were there with someone it doesn't concern so much."

Slowly she came toward me, smiling mysteriously. She looked me in the eyes. Then she took my hand and tenderly pushed it under her clothes—right onto her belly, which exuded warmth. My skin merged with her skin. "That is how much it concerns you," she said.

There was no time for more. We sat down together in the kitchen for bread and tea. "Have you found out anything new?" I asked Tomas.

"Nothing from the radio. But the professor believes that something will happen. During the last strike it was like this too, apparently."

Tomas was sitting next to Simeonu like some kind of adviser. At one point he even put his hand on the older man's shoulder and said: "If nothing happens, it won't be the end of the world, Professor." Mirela was pouring tea. "Thank you," I said. (She couldn't have known that I was the one who had seen her.)

I turned back to the professor: "I don't understand how you can expect people to gather so early in the morning."

"When else if not in the morning?" said the professor, puzzled.

The kitchen was full of anxiety. If we delayed we might miss something important—something we could not be allowed to miss. But none of us longed to strike out into what was still empty space and wander through the streets like someone who has mixed up the day, month, and season of the year and now stands in a bathing suit on a snow-covered meadow asking the passing skiers which way to the nearest beach. That's how we could have ended up because it wasn't certain that something would really happen.

The white-and-yellow tablecloth covered the parts of the sideboard where yesterday the group of workmen had been sitting. Their place was now empty. "Perhaps," I thought, "they haven't yet got in to work. They'll be back when the day has woken up completely."

Livie and I looked at each other. I had no inkling that

these indifferent moments would be almost our last. Her emaciated face—always softly glowing from the center of her forehead—had meanwhile become the face closest to me.

High in the mountains of this Country is a place where a small stream gushes from a pile of rocks. Around it on three sides are precipices and the fourth side drops slowly in a curve to the right. Now, in the winter, the snow is everywhere: even the spring is invisible and all that can be seen are the tips of the stones, bulging as if teased. One of the slopes ends a little further up in a short cliff, and behind it spreads a mountain plateau.

I have never been there and I never shall. But this will cause no change in its appearance. The sun will go on rising and casting a faint luster on the fallen snow. Or at other times mist will seal everything in its impenetrable cape. And as day turns into night the darkness will spread out as it has done all the days of my life.

The world has any number of such places. The tentacles of my destiny walk them instead of me. The tentacles of our destinies. Their steps can be heard over grass unmarked by our feet. Far behind our backs they resolve and determine. Sometimes to our contentment, at other times harshly, insensitively, cruelly. They are everywhere we are not—in this only are they close to us.

On this day the decision had already been made early, because it was called naked. Mme. Mirela's backside hung on its flagpole like a banner. And the decision had been made with a cruelty that cuts so sharply that at first a man does not feel it.

We went out into the street where the darkness was already thinning. Tentacles hung down from the invisible hills. I felt their indifferent swaying. Mirela did not come with us; we walked—Livie, Simeonu, Tomas, and I. It was still quite warm, but fundamentally colder than yesterday. If such weather had been consistent the snow would perhaps have continued to cover the city. But the last snow had thawed in the night rain. And so we waited for a new fall.

I felt an unaccustomed harmony with humanity. Everyone was aiming in what seemed indisputably the same direction. Here tramped a family with a boy and an old grandmother. There walked a worker and his wife. They exalted me, although they were not themselves exalted. Rather, desperately serious.

Their seriousness flowed together into a current. I moved at Livie's side and we hooked our arms together. We walked quickly, silently. Although it was damp, words were drying on our lips.

In front of us a military patrol appeared. As we slipped past it anxiety and a pugnacious excitement gripped me. But the patrol glanced at us without interest. So far we didn't figure in its instructions.

Our crowd thickened and and stretched out into the distance. Over the clouds, which were higher than yesterday's, the sunrise was on its way. I looked in its direction. Perhaps I was seeking white dove wings stretching out over us. What would I have given at least to see them glimmer between the indistinguishable wads of cloud. But an ominous emptiness accompanied our path. Everything had been left to human will.

Even Tomas succumbed to the universal tension and walked beside the professor, taciturn and grave. My hand wandered toward Livie's hip. Simeonu either didn't want to see or didn't see. I wondered whether it wasn't extortion on my part to show my intentions just at this moment.

"What intentions?" said my skeptical "I." "You haven't the faintest idea what you are going to do about her."

We had turned a corner and the houses here were black, as if from soot. My parents would probably have been amazed to see me walking here with these people. "Think it over, Martin," they would have said, full of anxiety. "There's no solution." Because everything we do has to have a solution. So in fact we only do the things we are familiar with already. . . . My love affairs until now had all been generally transparent. I had been able to see right to the bottom of these otherwise always more or less clear, well-integrated unions.

Tomas shifted over to my side: "Look, there's the one who interrogated us."

It was true: walking in the road a little way away from us was the man with the cat face. Now, when Tomas pointed him out to me, he seemed to me very conspicuous. But on my own I would never have noticed him.

For some time I had been wanting to urinate. "What if they catch me at the meeting, lock me up, and won't let me leave?" Meanwhile Cathead had vanished in the stream of people. His colleague—the one with the rhomboid head—was apparently nowhere near. But the mere possibility made me clench my fist.

Five closed military vehicles stood here in a row. People were passing between them, and the steel plates, although surrounded by a ring of bodies, remained an unconquerable fortress.

In a gap between the houses a small Orthodox church appeared. Around it were heaps of rubble from recently demolished houses. "I'll nip round the corner here."

Close up, the church resembled a nineteenth-century villa. I was completely incapable of understanding its plump, onion-dome cheeks. I walked round to the further side. Here a very young gypsy girl with a herd of children was rooting around in the garbage. Normally I would have made myself inconspicuous, looked about me and left. Now, however, I had no choice. I turned my face to the wall of the church—my backside toward her.

We spilled out into a large space. The entrance to the factory was designed like a triumphal arch with a three-hundred-meter assembly area. In front and to the left towered dirty factory halls. To the right stood no less dirty townhouses and behind it several equally dirty concrete housing blocks. It took me a while to orientate myself in such a strangely ugly area. In the front half the incoming crowds of people were piling up. Between them and the factory glittered the closed ranks of the military and from the other side, in the factory forecourt, stood yet more people. The sidestreets were partly blocked by military vehicles. The gigantic (perhaps marble) gates of the factory reared above it all toward the heavens that the authorities so hated.

"You see, they have come," said Livie to her father, moved and proud.

"But if you had left for the country," it struck me, "you wouldn't have been able to be here."

Simeonu shrugged, and spoke perhaps for the first time that morning: "I thought we might save our skins."

Each step now was a fulfillment of the Scripture. Livie pushed on further and further. Tomas looked at me uneasily behind her back. "I too would rather have stayed at the edge," I said.

Once again I caught the sweetish local smell. The thickening crowd hampered our progress forward. To be honest, when I looked at the people around me I was surprised they had come. Some seemed lacking in culture. But others looked as if they were recalling a vanished culture now, on this day.

I trod·on the foot of a bent old woman and immediately apologized. She resembled the one who had been selling chesspieces at the crossroads. Every piece sold meant small change in the apron pocket: that was all she knew. Or these country people here: they had certainly left a sheep and cow at home. It was really an unusual achievement for the government of the Country to have driven them all to this point. As their ranks thickened I had to brush against the lapels of their coats, and sometimes even their trousers. It obviously didn't bother them at all since they didn't move away and they pressed on me with all their weight. The touch of their bodies aroused feelings of disgust in me.

"Livie!" I shouted at last. "How far do you want to go?!"

She looked around and waited. I pushed through to her and placatingly caught her under the arm. "How much further do you want to go, for God's sake?"

But we were already standing at the head of the crowd. Over several dozen heads I looked into the irreconcilable faces of soldiers.

Nor, for their part, did the demonstrators in front here look interested in any kind of reconciliation.

Tomas and Simeonu finally reached us. From behind, an anonymous pressure built up. The people standing in the factory forecourt now began to chant something. Occasionally a hand was raised clenched into a fist.

My attention was once again attracted by the gigantic gate. On each side was a support formed by a marble obelisk pointing to the heights like a lighthouse or a plague column. Above, the two marble sections were connected only by a concrete bulwark to which an ordinary red placard had been glued.

I also noticed the wooden platform under the right column. It was raised about a meter from the ground, and some force of ill omen emanated from it. I scrutinized it more carefully and realized that it was a headquarters. From its vantage point three black coats coldly measured up the growing crowd. The fourth had a general's greatcoat and was explaining something to the gorillas surrounding him. I had to admit that the four of them, and also some of the soldiers, looked well built and distinguished here in this turmoil. Many of the workers looked like grotesque dwarves beside them.

One of the black civilians walked up and down the boards in the likeness of omnipresent death. The remaining two conversed with their hands clasped behind their backs. The one furthest away was Romu.

I remembered his fingers strangling me to the clatter of wheels. That time I had even felt his low eager breath. It was strange now to see him here fifty meters away, which meant, nonetheless, a distance incomparably greater.

"Look," I showed Livie, "that's the man I was talking about." She nodded. We were holding hands but in these tense moments she was not exclusively mine. Nor did my time now belong only to her.

Once again I felt the touch of alien bodies—this time more imperative than before. The pressure gradually mounted. I realized that I was caught from all sides. What if I started to feel sick? To push my way out of this place would take ten to fifteen minutes. But only with the greatest effort and with no possibility of return. On all sides the endless foreign crowd stretched out. I glanced upward toward the monotonous clouds. They rolled above the countryside and above the town and they brought no omens.

The feeling that I couldn't get away urged me to leave. Only by an effort of will did I prevent the feeling growing into a confused animal terror. I tried at least occasionally to make some space for myself by twisting my torso. But the bodies pressed on me and gently squeezed. As the pressure mounted they even edged between us. I held onto her with all my strength. I became afraid for my Livie.

Afraid for my brave fearless Livie. But I knew how close she was to childish dependency. Before my eyes I saw her lying on the floor in the bedroom bundled up in my sleeping bag, needing me so much, her eyes feverishly roaming the darkness.

My struggle for her was a silent unvoiced struggle with an olive-skinned workman. He was letting himself be pressed between us like a slab of matter. Tomas stood on the other side and the professor was out of sight. The pressure suddenly increased sharply. Over the workman's shoulder Livie threw me a glance I didn't dare to read. The people around started to chant something and pressed against my chest. I was overcome by weakness and a feeling of powerlessness. I held on to Livie with a twisted palm. Suddenly the ranks arched back and a roar sounded. "The soldiers are attacking," it struck me. My fingers lost their grip. Once more I glimpsed Livie's face over the workman's shoulder. Her clear blue eyes were saying good-bye.

Then I was seized by a living wave and carried back. I thought I was going to fall, but there was nowhere to fall. We became each other's prisoners—we, who had wanted; what was it we had really wanted?! "Please," I was saying tearfully to those who stood closest to me, "Give it up, please!"

Livie was overwhelmed by the torrent of swaying bodies. But I was carried away beyond recall. I heard myself making anxious noises and I wasn't standing on my feet at all. Immediately behind me a cordon of soldiers was beating its way through with batons. There was no hope of escape through the mass of compressed bodies. It was a perfect— because mutual—trap.

The people at the edges had evidently not been taken unaware like us and they had started fighting. The pressure let up a little. "Where shall I find her again?" echoed in my head, "Where shall I see her?" But I was seized by another wave. They had divided the demonstration into two halves and now they were driving mine away. I had to walk slowly to a destination unknown. From the other side of the square there were bursts of gunfire. Some woman started to scream more hysterically than before. The air flashed with the iron batons of the soldiers.

Suddenly the line broke and behind it—like a miracle— shone a street. In a frenzy I burst forward. As I ran I stumbled over someone who was trying to get up. Tomas appeared in front of me and we raced down the unending street. "Livie!" I shouted at him from behind, "Livie stayed back there somewhere!" But I kept on running.

Still, I did slow down a little and Tomas receded in the

distance ahead of me. I looked around and stopped at the nearest door. From the square came the racket of gunshots. The crowd streamed around me. But there were some people who were also stopping and helplessly looking for their friends and family. To go back was impossible, and so they could only hope that those they loved would suddenly emerge.

I would have given anything if she had only emerged. I was only half-saved—there was no reason to rejoice. If I had seen her I would have run to her wildly. If I had seen her it would have meant the abolition of misfortune, with retrospective effect.

I was choking with longing, uncertainty, and pain. Again and again her eyes returned to me as they said good-bye. The gunfire ceased, the crowd thinned, and a few of us remained waiting. People were now only walking—broken by what they had seen—as if deprived of will and with extinguished eyes. Occasionally somebody supported another; women were allowing themselves to be led. One man, who was still waiting, could have been about my age. He had his flat cap pulled down over his forehead and he fixed each approaching girl closely with an unbelieving stare. One stopped and with tears in her eyes looked back. The man in the flat cap gazed at her in fellow feeling. Then he asked her something and took her hand. They left together without belonging to each other; I remained alone.

II

Once again I turned back toward the square. Between the armored vehicles glittered patches of color. I tried in vain to see more. "Maybe I ought to go there," I thought. "Is this the moment for throwing caution to the winds, or not yet?"

But my skeptical "I" rushed to my aid this time and said: "They won't let you go there, anyway."

"And what if she's lying there deserted by everybody?" I exclaimed.

"If she's lying there, then she'll lie there with you too. You can't help her!"

"But that's so horribly cruel: not to be able to help her. Or Simeonu." It struck me only then. "And after all, it's useless to talk about love with someone who doesn't know what love is about."

I turned my head away from those inexplicable patches and started to run. I ran home hoping the others would go there too, because they too would be afraid for me. It was really my only sensible thought. And so I ran, and as I ran my despair grew with my growing hope.

At the end of the street the crowd was massing once again. Some people had paving-stones in their hands. At that moment they didn't interest me.

I was threading my way through the still sparse sieve of the newly forming throng. If I could only get behind them—into empty space. At that moment a shopwindow smashed and glass shattered into a thousand fragments. I heard the angry shouts of people. No, they didn't interest me. Only one thing, perhaps: the heaps of scattered splinters reminded me of Livie. Just like her they smiled tenderly and gravely in the middle of a dank grayness. I realized that the most important word, the word she had waited and wanted to hear, was one that I had still not spoken.

I pushed on. What I hadn't managed to say earlier was now almost screaming from my lips: "Livie, I'm determined to live with you anyway in the world." I should have said it the night before, in their attic. Or immediately she had let fall her "in the end you will leave anyway"—such alien words. But I had pushed her away at first and then—up there—I had said, "When I finally go home." Home. How could I have believed that it wouldn't wound her?

"In the end you will leave anyway." Something cracked

and a terrifying pain poured out of the words like pus. I begged that sometime I would be able to atone for her suffering. But her eyes were saying good-bye to me.

The street came to an end and I ran to the right through a long alley. Barbed wire wound along the crest of the fence ahead. I realized I was in this place for the third time. The first time had been when Tomas and I were trying to leave the town. The second had been before the destruction of the professor's demands. Today the alley was full of people. But the smooth tree trunks struck upward toward ever more desolate heights. And all the snow had vanished. I understood that its disappearance was linked to Livie.

At the corner of a park the demonstrators were demolishing some office or other. The soldiers were obviously concentrated at the entrances to the factories and more important offices and here they were not prepared. Here there was room for a few gulps of freedom—even if only in the form of destruction. But everything had already been decided and the destruction only preceded the approach of bondage and despair. There wasn't even so much blood. It was more that the thongs were tightening through the town and where they cut into the flesh, were coloring with blood.

Another crash. Perhaps it would enable its author to endure the next month of bondage. But what about me? My life was crumbling before the possibility of the irreversible and final. "God, nothing matters, only that she doesn't suffer."

And so the people passing me saw a man fully immersed in his own misfortune, a man whose eyes and mind and everything else aimed through some narrower street. I got as far as the place where Augusto Cudean lived. Here it was relatively calm. The soldiers had already placed their sentries here much earlier. Behind the fence glittered something white. I stepped, unbelievingly, nearer. It was a little heap of snow but it glittered nevertheless. Again I felt an unknown link with her. Children had obviously built a snowman here some time ago; in the little cake that was left the outspread arms could still be recognized; snow merged with mud and continued to thaw. But I felt the link with her. The last, truly the last, snow. The last living snowman in this town. The last bell. How had it been when she had heard the last bell at school? The fur coat she wore when I first saw her gave off a beautiful warmth.

The clouds were so shapeless today that viewed from the bottom of the street it was not clear if the sky was gray or the cloud blue. Coming after dark and windy days this might seem a change for the better but I saw it the other way around: the world looked at me with a nothing-doing sour smile and I was losing my very self in its indifference. It reminded me of my native land.

I drew nearer to the North-South Road. On the opposite corner men in overcoats were beating some unfortunate. The beaten man fell to the ground and the three kicked him with unbelievable cruelty. Anyone could have been in his place: even me. I realized that Livie would never be safe here. I longed for some new—third—country, in which I could live with her. Yes, that would surely be a solution.

"There is no third country," my skeptical "I" told me, "where they would admit both you and her. You should know: the servants without form and face, no more than screws in the wheels of power, have claimed the right to human destinies. Your story is their property, absurd as it is."

"I don't care! I don't care at all!" I shouted. Because even the finest-tuned mechanism loosens in the end. I shall wait until it loosens. If necessary I shall wait half my life, only let her come back.

"You're saying that now because the threat to her has out-weighed all the others. But when she's next to you your indecision will revive again."

The screams of the man who had been dragged off died somewhere in the courtyard, and once again I trembled at the thought of it and at the memory of the terrifying grasp of the crowd whose victim I could have been. Nobody was waiting for me in front of entrance no. 1023.

The image of Mirela appeared to me suddenly. I went inside unprepared for a confrontation with her. "Yes," I realized, "if I'm the first to get here I shall have to tell her something." I swallowed nervously. Only now did I recall the worry on her features when she had walked us to the door. She had probably been afraid to be afraid, thinking that this would spoil our enthusiasm. Wretched Mirela. Why hadn't she come with us? What value would it have for her to survive the others?

But no, they still wouldn't have taken her along. And her tears had been kept well hidden under her eyelids: "Wait for us here, mummy, you can read something." It was difficult to say which alternative would have been worse for a mother.

I climbed up the stairs and inside me my heart was beating—a shy bird. I knew that with each step a piece of hope was deserting me. And by the time I stood at their door, the decision had been made for that moment, even though I had not yet admitted it to myself. I was standing at this door alone.

Suddenly something clicked and Mirela appeared without my ringing the bell. Her face, emptied almost to impassiveness, terrified me. She must have had an inkling of what had happened in the square. Her half-absent gaze passed by me and slid toward my nonexistent companions. Only then did she focus on me and, surprised at whom she saw, she asked me something in the local language. Under her eyes were great dark bags.

"They will certainly come," I tried to gesticulate, "you needn't be afraid." And when she failed to understand, I pointed to a time segment on my wristwatch. "When this has gone by, they will certainly show up. We must wait. Wait." I gave an encouraging smile.

She let me slip in past her. Again she asked something. I

didn't understand her. I took my shoes off and she vanished. While I took my shoes off, the zinc washbasin was looking in the opposite direction. The light had also averted its eyes. One thing was certain: "Nobody else is here. Nobody."

I felt immeasurably guilty that I was the only one here. Hesitatingly I entered the room. But it was full of workmen. They occupied every corner: they were propping their arms on the tabletop or staring up into emptiness. Mirela was sitting among them turned somewhere inward—as if nothing remained here that still belonged to her. The unconscious relaxation of the workers gave the opposite impression of sovereign, if unsought, ownership.

I took a step and followed the workmen with a sidelong glance. Two of them were small, with dark wrinkled faces. The other two were familiar to me. The sturdiest was probably the boss. Yesterday, sitting on the sideboard, he had looked the same.

Through the window a little light was falling, illuminating this curious siesta. From the bookcase stared the ranks of books, growing deaf and changing into printed piles of paper. Above, on the shelf, stood the candlestick. It seemed to me that its brass blood was slowly flowing out. But when I caught its eye a sudden fear for Livie ran through us both. "She is so good," we both thought. And into both our minds came a complete picture of her—as we loved her.

Something flickered and was again extinguished. "What is the meaning of all this?" I said.

"I don't ask what it means when I suffer," replied the candlestick. "Joy and weeping come like sun and rain into the world of men."

A common sadness united us. After a moment the candlestick breathed in and continued: "I don't think that suffering should be some special good fortune. And the unceasing icy rain will not warm human hearts. But the land that has moisture enough is blessed."

"A parable?" I was taken aback. "Who among us will take

pleasure in such a parable? Whom will it help in misfortune? I'd rather hear what precisely you are going to do!"

"What I'm going to do? I shall be just a piece of brass— an alloy of copper and zinc—curiously molded. I no longer have any other goal."

"Don't you long to save yourself?"

"I don't."

The candlestick spoke wearily and quietly. I considered its temperament and mood. I knew that I didn't have much time to persuade it. "Look at that radio," I pointed downward, "look at its tinny grin. It was created that way, for idiotic grinning. But when its moment comes it will do anything to survive. It will emit hideous, senseless noises. Ever more hideous. In the end almost incomprehensible noises. All of them just to be able to live."

"Living and surviving are not the same thing," said the candlestick.

I saw it growing colder in front of my eyes. "Now you are taking me too literally," I said.

The candlestick was startled and it obviously didn't feel like saying anything more. Then it gathered the last drop of patience and strength left to it. "He who wants to grin can go on grinning for all I care," it declared in a steady voice. "I shall stand here silent as long as they let me. Perhaps until the time when the language of communication in the world becomes silence." It shuddered imperceptibly. "It is needful to build the new Jerusalem," it whispered. "And that is all."

As it spoke these words, the brass smoothed out and hardened almost antagonistically. Our conversation was over. Between the workmen sat Mirela—she who carried this blood and had passed it on to Livie. She sat between them, unrecognized, unrevealed. Her absent gaze drew her away from them and toward the center of that Country that both was and was not her homeland—the place where her belly, breasts and womb spread out. It was her only escape route.

I went into the kitchen almost surprised to be alone. This time I wasn't taken aback to find yet another group of diggers. I continued on into the hall, which was empty and almost dark. I wondered when Tomas, at least, would return. After all, he had been running down the same street. Once again I was reminded of that terrifying crush. And the murderous longing of each to live, even at the expense of the others.

The past two days were winding backward like a long woeful life lived with Livie. I wished her a happiness that would reach right up to the tears on her sharp tender face. I wandered around the empty bedrooom. But I could find no rest. I returned to the hall and put my shoes on. On the coatrack hung the fur coat once worn by the father, Simeonu Cudean. I walked out into the corridor and just that moment Tomas arrived. He had already reached the landing below and was smiling happily.

"Didn't you hear me calling," I asked, "when we were running?"

"No," he said, surprised. He ran up the last steps and breathed quickly. "And where are the others?"

My answer was an anxious silence.

"They still haven't come back?"

" . . . . "

"And in there . . . ?" He pointed, now with complete gravity, to the door.

"I wouldn't go in there if I were you," I said.

He considered. His face and the islet forming in the pale growth of his hair were red from haste. "Well, . . . it doesn't mean anything yet. They could easily be coming."

"I know. But what do you want to do?"

Once again he considered. "I would wait half an hour or so and then we could go and see what's going on."

I considered his words. Again I was dealing with some kind of mask I couldn't penetrate, but it contributed to meaningful activity. "You're right," I said.

The day that had begun with the bare backside of Mme. Mirela could be called nothing other than naked day. But Mme. Mirela was now sitting swallowed up in herself on the topmost floor of a house where, working in the basement, there was probably a gang of diggers exactly like those who surrounded Mirela and veiled her bottomless solitude. We two, Tomas and I, walked out of the house. It did not even surprise us when the man with the cat face emerged from a nearby black car. He opened the rear door and ordered us to get in. It was even helpful in one respect—it gave us hope that we would meet the professor and Livie.

The car door slammed behind us and in the man at the wheel I recognized the lanky individual with the rhomboid head—that abortive Slovak who had interrogated us. But the house was already rushing away, together with the North-South Road specked with returning demonstrators whose broken, shocked faces flashed past behind the bullet-proof glass. Lanky drove very surely and the wings of my hatred for him were clipped by my awareness that we were only character actors in somebody's play—a somebody who had already determined the script for us, and for everyone. I had a premonition that I would soon stand face to face with him.

They drove us first north and then east. We rode round the factories on the side that faced away from the town. The world outside became unbelievably remote, not because it was definably alien, but because for the next, as yet uncircumscribed moments, it was not meant for us.

The murmur of events receded and only what was meaningful remained with us. This was Simeonu, Livie, Mirela; even Andrei, absent and angry, emerged from unbetrayed hiding places. Scuttling like mice under the seat were my parents, waiting in Prague. Outside, the houses moved apart for a moment and the steep hillsides appeared, nearer and darker than ever before. Behind the wheel Lanky fixed his concentrated gaze forward, his companion threw an arm across the back of his seat, and they both seemed utterly disgusted by us.

I saw a mother and child and the sight brought to my mind the two country mothers with their infants tied to their bodies in the underpassage of the station. The future was pulsating obscurely in the shadow of the past. Here was the goblin from the train, the two pilgrims—so different from each other yet waiting hand in hand under the leafless apple tree; then the dove, the candlestick, the grey uniforms of the diggers. In the last place, Tomas, silent beside me.

Once again blackened trees appeared above the high, and in this part of town, the only wooden houses. Someone hirsute was walking along the pavement opposite us; when he saw us, he looked back at the car in surprise and fear, and slowly disappeared in the distance. It struck me that in everybody here there was a little of Remu, and I knew that somewhere ahead Remu was waiting for us and for everyone. And he who had determined the script also knew it, and frowned ominously at the reverse-side of things.

Our captors continued to say nothing and perhaps didn't even know what to say to us. The chief with the face conspicuous for its cat features lit up a cigarette; a police silence reigned—a little oppressive and a little embarassing in its intimacy, a silence in which one sort of animal restricts another for no reason.

We drove into a broad courtyard. "Yet another shack," I thought. I slid out of the car and onto a pavement that resembled the one where the bloodshed had taken place and my dear ones too had vanished. The extent of the calamity was something that I still couldn't grasp, even now—since all that I had seen and felt had been the mass of bodies closing on me, and the screaming and the sound of gunfire.

The courtyard was partially open onto the street, and

bordered on the right side by an apartment house and on the left only by a rural cottage. To my surprise they took us into the apartment house. First the chief, then Tomas, and then Lanky and me. "Now we'll see," I thought. "I should ask about Livie here."

We started to climb up and on the first floor an iron grille blocked the steps. A giant guard opened it. When we were walking past him he stretched his wrestler's arms. I was beginning to hope that I wouldn't meet Livie here. To have come here as a citizen of this Country must have been appalling.

"You are only a spectator, a spectator!" exclaimed my skeptical "I." "You believe your nationality will protect you!"

"Doesn't every man," I said, "believe that simply because he's been used to safety he'll somehow save himself? That he'll get away with it, one more time?"

And when my skeptical "I" remained silent, aware of its share of truth, I continued: "Over there in the courtyard, where we got out of their car, we probably had our last chance to save ourselves by flight. But even if I'd been from this Country, I certainly wouldn't have run for it. A man can always finds some reason or other until he takes the downward path, alone and of his own free will. Just as Andrei has taken it."

We had already climbed up to the third floor. Along the shaft of the lift ran a monotonous banister. Everywhere a surprising calm. Tomas went ahead of me, sunk deep into himself. I had never seen him like that. We turned away from the staircase and the man who had determined the script came nearer. Chill: a short corridor full of seams. A single window and behind it the courtyard. "No look!" ordered the Slovak. But I wasn't looking. What's in the courtyard doesn't interest me. "How stupidly they feast on us." I think, "What would they do in our shoes?" We are at the end of the corridor. Once again I realize that I am responsible to the professor and to Livie. But my accustomed feeling of safety is leaving me. I feel helpless. I will never, never see her again.

Romu was sitting at a desk in the otherwise empty room. He was wearing warm, worn-out clothes and there was absolutely nothing special about him. I was suddenly almost uncertain that it was him. When he saw us he got up and went over to the window. On the way he issued several orders. I wondered why, when the majority of the nation were so short, there were so many exceedingly tall people here. The medium range was missing.

The Slovak and the chief sat down. All the time I felt drawn by the chief's sweetish face, impenetrable as big cats' faces are. Again and again I reveled in its strangeness.

I silently communicated with Tomas. Both of us still remembered Romu's gloomy form pacing above the heads of the crowd, demonic and beautiful. He had been swathed in mystery—whether on the wooden scaffolding or behind the curtain of the Restaurant Europa or in front of the pink house—in all the places where he had remained hidden. But now at last he turned round and I remembered that entirely different expression of his, the expression from the train corridor, full of limitless lust. Perhaps only Remu had been able to slow him down, and strangely enough, he did so by pure lack of constraint. Did Romu have some incomprehensible weakness for this quality, a weakness bordering on closeness?

Lanky got up and walked through the room. Romu pulled out an elongated piece of paper. At the top the word "Restaurant" was printed. The number 23—underlined—was scrawled under it and beneath a line was the total: 123. It was the bill from the Restaurant Europa. But with a hundred added on.

"Pay!" shouted Lanky.

Tomas hunted in his pockets and dug about in them for some time. At last he found the two blue banknotes. In the currency of the Country each had the value of one hundred.

Romu triumphantly crumpled them in his palm and stuffed them into his pocket. He looked us over with satisfaction and now seemed to have grown bigger in his own estimation. After a while he nodded toward the door. His gesture, however, was full of the generosity of somebody who was not, in any case, saying a final good-bye. From the first meters of this Country he had been tied to us. From our first steps beyond the border wire he had emerged. Now he had deliberately confirmed his determination to take part in our destiny.

The doors behind us slammed. "Excuse me!" I blurted at Lanky, "Excuse me, I need to ask about someone—some people I know." He brushed it off and pushed us aside as if he hadn't heard.

"But I really need to ask about something," I shouted. In proof of the seriousness of my intent I pulled out my Czechoslovak passport. "Ask!" I said.

Lanky lost his confidence. I looked him in the eye: "Livie Cudean, Simeonu Cudean!" He shrugged and shook his head at my persistence. "These two escaped with their skins," he probably thought, "and they're still not satisfied." "Livie Cudean," I repeated. At this moment the commander rasped something and they both mercilessly marched us out. Neither Tomas nor I dared to resist. As we walked, from somewhere inside came the sound of sighing and the dull thud of blows.

IV

"Did you understand it?" asked Tomas, when they had let us out onto the pavement below.

"I didn't."

Scarcely a breath of wind blew through the street and the clouds on the horizon presaged new rain or snow. Nothing but emptiness in us. "Perhaps they're home by now," I said.

"They could be."

"You're only saying that to please me."

"No, I'm not. Why shouldn't they be home?" he countered. "After all, we don't know how things work here."

We didn't turn round, and walked on. Nobody was standing at the trolley stop. The line was number 36. It was obvious that it hadn't been running for some time.

We veered away from the town and the factory walls. Here—in remote districts, half-village and half-town—was calm. The suspicious eyes of children followed us from inside rooms.

"We ought to go home," said Tomas.

"You can't be serious!" I cried. And more mildly I added: "It's just not possible."

"What do you want to do?" he asked.

I said nothing.

"Now they'll always be following us," he went on.

"They certainly will." A chill ran down my spine. "Sometimes it feels as if they've grown a part of us."

"Precisely."

"But look here!" I stopped in my tracks. "That's part of it. It's a way of life here." For a second he seemed convinced and confused. Then he started up again immediately. "Anyway, we only came here for a week. Remember how many days have already gone by. What can you achieve in the few days we still have?"

A short, merciless fight was taking place in me. "These are new days," I declared. "And a time other than before. Even if we haven't managed to enter it yet. But one thing is certain: we have lost our way. Home no longer exists. But it's also possible that we no longer exist."

We turned back. From the center came the sound of several volleys of gunfire—as if children had placed caps under the tramwheels. From one spot thick black smoke was climbing above the houses. A whiff of smoke floated from the distance together with the sound.

We crossed over the North-South Road. Here, standing

in small knots, were men the soldiers had pushed out of the small park. A motionless body appeared, washed up here like a scrap of paper. Organ music failed to sound and the resignation of nonbeing flowed common and nameless into the bones. I dug my fingernails through my pocket into my thighs. Poor Livie. Why did she do everything wholly? She couldn't stay just on the edge of the square; she had to get herself into the center. She couldn't just long for warmth; she had to radiate it. She couldn't just love me a little; she had to belong to me. She couldn't even leave us her body; a gray vestige. She had to leave us wholly.

We trod on. Before us loomed the pink house. In the entrance passage it was gradually growing dark. An image of the dogged workmen flashed through my mind. I realized that if Livie had returned without her father she would be alone with them in the flat.

The final steps on the stairs. A growing anxiety within me. It would seem that I believe in miracles, but I do not. I am empty. I feel the house trembling from its foundations. On the second floor Tomas gropes for the switch and a weak bulb lights the staircase from top to bottom. I manage to walk up to one more landing. He is five steps higher. I stop. "You said they could be home. You said so!"

Tomas was mute with surprise.

"Answer me! Did you or didn't you say so?"

"Well, I did."

I overtook him angrily, as if he were to blame for everything. "I only want to know whether you still think so."

The door to the apartment is ajar. We are opening it. In the hallway sitting on a chair is Mirela. Around her on the floor lie our things and some of hers. Everything here huddles as if in exile. The room are shut. The whole scene is almost too eloquent an answer.

"We have to do something," says Tomas, under the influence of what he sees.

I nod.

But Mirela is rising and in her hand she holds a large book. It is a dictionary. Some pages are marked. Mirela approaches us with limitless and irrefutable prejudice. She is as old as life on this earth; she is even older. She is at the end. Her physical height is like a cross hastily nailed together. One by one she shows us the prepared German words: "you," "leave," "husband," "daughter," "return." At first I do not understand and then I stiffen, because I see that she believes it. I look into her inflamed eyes. In them there is not an ounce of detachment nor an ounce of sympathy with us. We believe that as foreigners we can achieve something. That at the very least we are protecting our hosts simply by our presence. But who would dare to oppose this woman— a mother. It would be like ignoring her last wish. Although, on the other hand, are we obliged to submit to a demand so obviously pointless? We are incapable of words and everything is churning in our heads. "Tomas," I stutter, finally, "this is terrible. She thinks that everything is our fault."

And Mirela is already pointing at other words: "you," "stay," "danger," "for," "we," "you," "leave," "away." She doesn't care what we think, she doesn't care that she was once hospitable. She has one fixed vision and she clings to it. Once again Tomas and I exchange glances. We too are at the end. We have nothing to say to her.

"We shall have to go," we say, in the end, almost simultaneously. Eloquently we stand by our things. Mirela is at our back. Now that she has triumphed, she apologizes. If only she chose to say nothing. If she would only shut up, for God's sake!

We pack up. Suddenly I drop the sleeping bag on the floor. "Fuck it all!" I kneel over it all strength spent. Then I go on tightening the straps of the backpack. I feel like a betrayer. I would never have believed that I could be forced into such a betrayal. If only someone knew what had happened between me and her. But I had known her so briefly. No human institution exists in whose eyes she belongs to me.

At last we are packed. It only remains to get up and leave. I notice that Mirela has also piled up quite a few things. Some clothes, toiletries, a trunk, even a blanket. As if she had just moved into the hallway. The apartment behind the doors to the rooms is silent. I shall never find out if the gang of workers is sitting in the living room. If there are still more of them. If even Livie's room is flooded with their grayness. It's time to leave this place. We get up and exchange good-byes with Mirela. I see that she is more ashamed than it might look, but this does nothing to change the whole situation. We walk toward the exit with no knowledge of our fate in the next minutes and days. We step into the entrance passage, where there are only a few meters to the attic. Once again I long for everything to return. For it to be only the day before yesterday and we, healthy and frozen, just entering the door with suitcases. But we are going away—forever.

THE DANCE OF THE WOLVES

I

AN IRON GRILLE WAS YET AGAIN RUNNING FROM EAST TO west, driven by the rolling lava-stream of clouds. While in the west the red glow of afternoon was returning the December mist to the lowlands, above the mountains it was growing dark and above us a sharp divide had formed. An icy drizzle was beginning.

"Look," Tomas pointed. "That cloud over there looks like a wolf's paw."

As soon as he said it, the sound of hungry canine howling came from somewhere, immediately followed by the growl of a truck engine. It tore down on us along the road.

"Be careful," I shouted, "some patrol." In my imagination I saw ourselves sprayed with a magazine of lead. But instead, a young soldier on the back waved to us cheerlessly. The back of the truck was full of such soldiers.

I looked beyond the vehicle and it seemed to me that the drizzling dimness was disclosing a figure who remained hidden. In the meantime the wolf paw had spread and formed itself into demonically unbound shapes, and now it was reaching from us to the gloomy ramparts of the mountains. I recalled the too generous gesture with which Romu had released us through the door. I strained my eyes as much as I could to see if I could still catch a glimpse of him. But I could see nothing—only the droplets of his omnipresence drifting into the unpeopled spaces. The road was iced with them and was now smooth, silvery, and glistening. People were discovering with surprise that they were still alive, and were slipping away. We stepped out ahead. I went first—with a rolling gait—I carried excessive ballast on my back. And if fate had possessed a horizon, I would have been gazing into the distant chasm of that horizon from which, despite all emptiness, there rose shapes mysterious and curious. The idea of the railway station, however, did not cross my mind.

Someone's wounded laughter cut through the yellow monotony of a barracks-like dormitory. I pointed over a fence at a Formica cabin. Between two poles hung a swing on a rope. Scattered below it lay a trowel, a little tractor and a handkerchief. "And I'd thought that this was a quarter of soldiers, plum brandy, and gypsies. And it's a children's quarter."

"Don't stop!" something told me, and I trod on. As the integrity of the older built-up area disappeared, it became impossible to recall the Cudean family. Lost too was their house with its undermined walls rising up into nothingness. The pack on my back grew still heavier—it was clear that it had been badly, too rapidly, packed.

"What a shambles," I hissed. I now walked on more quickly, I hurtled through my own demolition-site, waiting to see what would be born. And meanwhile my parents in Prague were just preparing for supper. And meanwhile the December evening had drifted down at Charles Bridge over the Vltava. And meanwhile Livie had laid my palm on her belly, but that belly had departed and is lost. Her belly, my fragile country. Whose was the laughter from the dormitory?

I recall the warmth that flowed from her at the moment of touch. What had she really communicated to me? Did she by any chance mean . . . ? I prefer to break off the thought and walk—even run away. "Where to, really?" challenged Tomas. "I don't know," I say, "you can see, after all, that we must go!"

Our journey has no goal. It doesn't even have a reason; only the necessity of going. "This is how much it concerns you," she had said. If I think it right through, I ought to weep all night. But I am not capable of tears; I am a traitor, helpless. Droplets of water run down my face instead of tears.

I feel the discomfort of the sodden path leading alongside the road. Absolutely nobody lives in these outlying areas. By morning everything will be frozen; perhaps there will be snowfall. I look at myself and discover that my heart is a pump. I feel that I am being followed. I turn round, but once again I can see no one. To the right is a fence, and nearby grass, a footpath, again grass, a roadway. A man who knows the future does not overexert himself. He drifts on across the earth in gusts of freezing droplets.

The last crossroads. Soon we shall walk into the fields. Opposite stands a patrol vehicle. Under the tarpaulin is a light.

We walk past the vehicle and wait for something to break. But absolutely nothing moves and the distance to the fields remains the same. Close behind my heels in the road yawns a deep precipice—a crevice. It is two meters wide. One step would be enough and I would have ended where the fixed gaze finds no horizon. The scar runs almost alongside the road, and so five paces take me less than half a meter from its edge, which is on my left hand.

Darkness has completely fallen; clouds have spread out across the sky, devoid of any form. My left arm (the heart arm) dangles toward the precipice as if toward a grave. With my right hand I grasp the strap and pull my backpack as close as possible to my body. Cold creeps from the side.

"What are you really doing here?" I ask Tomas. "You wanted to go back, after all."

"I'll finish in three days," he replies.

THE DANCE OF THE WOLVES

I think: "How can such dumb thoughts occur to you?" But I say nothing out loud.

At the edge of the precipice sits a mottled-gray tomcat, licking itself. I stamp my foot and the cat makes off, but the depths begin to vibrate—as if concealing a nest of wasps. A rumbling has risen to the very edge of the chasm, but I too am ascending, and not long after, I am in the embrace of an incomprehensibly stout cloud. It's the beginning of the dance of the wolves as they float into the distance. Without waiting a moment longer I mount the nearest back. The fur opens up like a ball of steam. I bury my face in it and stroke it with my own cheek. The wolves' eyes shine, but there's no way to read, either in them or in smiles too strangled. "You know what?" I say, to bridge the gap. "Let's all make an unfulfillable wish." Nobody accepts my game—understandably, since the wish I subconsciously have in mind is one that can be fulfilled. I feel as if I had let something out, but the wolves keep up their gallivanting and their expressionless faces swim around me. I abandon the first back, turn around after them, try to catch them by their tails. Without a sign of interest they escape. Once again I try it, but they spring away like balloons. To crown everything, the sky seals us in a cape of darkness. Independent of me the wolves recede into it, and again return. Finally I realize they are aiming under a torn rock where, from an ice-covered plateau, grows a mountain spruce with green-blue lichen on its perfumed bark. I understand, because this direction is the trajectory of my heart and at its end is reunion. "Why are you so good, my darling wolves," I say, while stretching out my palm into ever-thickening drizzle; my hair is wet, and even my scarf is sodden. The rumbling gets stronger and becomes deafening. A big truck is stopping just beside us. How it got here is beyond my understanding. The engine idles; the cabin with doors ajar vibrates. We climb in and the colossus sets off. But even now the faces of the wolves don't change—they float into a distance given once and for all time—with tongues hanging out, with dull flames in their mica eyes.

II

The headlights, turned down to minimum, slice into darkness for no more than a few meters ahead. The driver nervously turns his head. He is leaning on the wheel as if on the neck of a galloping steed. So far we have not spoken. But still, glances say so much. The cabin is full of them, even flatulent with them. A wheel bounces in a depression; we all jump up and then sit down as before. We jump several times in succession. Somewhere behind us the town recedes—the town encountered only a few days before. I realize the irreversibility of this retreat and am taken aback by it. I am truly leaving without having learned what happened to Livie. I am going and leaving behind me an unfinished story. This then, finally, is the face of good-bye.

"You're moved!" my skeptical "I" shouts at me. "You're easily moved. But you still won't open the door and run back with all your strength! You won't stop a bayonet with your own chest! You won't file through prison bars."

"File through bars, when she isn't behind them? What would be the point?"

"The point would be that you wouldn't be behaving like a calculating Central European. Or don't you love her any more?"

"Livie? She is half of me."

"You see then."

"What do I see? Even in places other than Central Europe people are afraid. They are afraid of foolish things, because they pause to reflect."

"Or maybe because they are cowards." My skeptical "I" cannot be shaken off.

I have no other arguments. "Everything was predetermined," I sigh. Behind the window a whitewashed building flashes past. "And then also . . . " The gang of diggers rises before my eyes. The cellar around them is covered with red dust. Cold yawns icily below the undermined walls. "And then Mirela too."

"What about Mirela?"

"She entirely disarmed me."

"Down!" the driver suddenly gestures. Nevertheless I catch a glimpse of a motorcycle parked at the roadside, a white helmet, and a red light in somebody's hand. I crouch with Tomas in a pile of rags. The driver stops and passes some documents out. Cigarettes as well. He is completely calm and this calms us too. They haggle over something in the local language. The documents are back in the cabin once again. The colossus starts up.

"Up," gestures the driver after a moment. He thumbs backward and waves a fist.

Once more we are silent for a while. We bounce over bumps and potholes.

"Polska?" he mutters through his teeth.

We shake our heads. "Czechs."

"Czechs," he repeats. His swarthy face gives nothing away.

We drive through the first village. Outside there is a continuous thick drizzle, but the mud on the roadsides is no longer melting. Water is gradually changing into snow.

"Where do you think he's taking us?" asks Tomas.

"Maybe the mountains," I answer. But it is quite possible that he is taking us somewhere else entirely—some faraway towns, villages, or even factories or storehouses. I give him a searching look. His documents were in order, it is true. But still they are like outlaws, he and the colossus that he commands. Like outlaws they struggle with the foul weather, the times, and the darkness on the poorly maintained—perhaps even closed—highways. The driver's searching eyes sometimes wander to the back mirror. And when he sees the darkness he is calm for a while.

The rear windshield. I would rather not look at it. I'm afraid that at any moment a dear face will appear in it. I'm afraid that it will be white and twisted out of recognition.

The highway is now ascending sharply. The cabin—an island of safety—is shaking ever more violently. We are pushing through the unknown country around us. Behind the window flash clumped shapes—suggestions of pastures, trees, dilapidated buildings. By the buildings there are usually fences of hewn logs. On one such log sits Lanky, looking in front of him—that means toward us. His figure flashes in the beam of light and disappears again.

"Did you see!?" I cry out, so that even the driver starts.

"What was there?"

"Lanky was there—the one who interrogated us. It was him for sure."

"That's just nonsense." Tomas exclaims angrily. "You couldn't have recognized him in this darkness."

"So explain to me who would be sitting outside on a soaking log in this shitty weather."

"So . . . water doesn't bother those people?" says Tomas wonderingly. And he continues placatingly: "Martin, it's more likely that some country man would be used to water. And then, here in this terrible Country everybody looks like everybody else."

"But that one certainly wanted us to notice him. When somebody is sitting on a wet freezing log, everyone notices him."

Tomas finally gives it some thought: "Well, . . . it's true that they could be following us. But how would they know we'd have got this far?"

"That's just the point. They know. The swine know it very well. And it seems that it suits them very well this way."

The highway turns upward in a curve. Asphalt has long ago been replaced by stone. We are bearing away from the direction of our ride up to now. Just like the driver I now follow the darkness behind us to check that it is inviolate.

Already there is no trace of the town: not the slightest vestige of original relationships. Nothing. I realize that in my hands I have nothing.

Nothingness splashes on the slope—timeless, eternal. Some especially high waves break on our vehicle from the side. And one time—perhaps very soon—they will toss the truck into the ditch and entirely deluge us. Then Romu will seize us by our throats and his face will be primitive, brutal, and licentious. But in these moments it is dangerously sublime and beautiful.

And here it dawns on me: "Why so many fears? Who cares about us?" And I begin, just a little—despite everything—to look forward to going outside.

The highway straightens again and outside the powdered snow is piling in innumerable drifts. It barely reaches the soles but it is mounting up. A number of houses appear, scattered on both sides. Their togetherness is unbelievably calming. The small windows shine free of all tension. "Look," I say to Tomas, "Christmas passed this way."

III

We drove around a church through an untouched square. Despite this I could not fail to notice an armored car. We came to a crossroads behind the village and there we stopped. The driver opened the door on our side and he climbed out as well. Frost whipped through the cabin. Numb and confused, we dropped to the ground and snow crunched under our feet. The driver gestured toward the route that wound ahead between the last group of buildings. He had already swung himself back up. I looked at him and I knew that this was the very last opportunity to find out where he had come from into the woeful night and where he was heading along the darkened roads. And he, as if he understood, pointed to himself and then somewhere obliquely to the right and downward, and the gesture told me that after today there was no longer any wherefrom or even any whereto for him, that there was only a withdrawal, further and further. And with that we made an end.

We two were left alone at the silent crossroads. I felt how the ground beneath my feet was hard, frozen solid.

"Tomas, does this Country really seem to you absolutely terrible?"

"Why?"

"After all, you said: here in this terrible Country every one resembles everybody else."

"And you don't find it terrible? You, of all people?"

"You're right." I looked down, ashamed, between our backpacks. We were trembling with cold. "Come on, we can't stay here."

We walked along the road that led between the last houses. There was really much more light than had at first appeared. The flakes were now falling sporadically and somewhere behind the clouds perhaps the moon was sailing, swollen to the bursting point. The countryside was torpidly translucent. We took down our backpacks so that we could put on more clothes. In front rose a high peak, topped with rocks—the beginning of a ridge. To the left lay its lower wooded shoulder. A second ridge ran ahead to the right— gentler and entirely wooded but ultimately perhaps no less high. The road led through a broad valley basin between the two ridges. Where we stood the basin was a kilometer wide and the extremities of the ridges did not rise above its floor by more than five hundred meters on the left and three hundred meters on the right. Masses of snow lay in spectral indifference on the rocks above. And despite the fact that this was an inaccessible alien world, it seemed to be within reach. A chill of longing ran through my chest; if she could only see it with me.

It was a Country as if created for withdrawal.

Once again it began to snow thickly and visibility decreased. A fine, cutting snow was falling. Silenced by our own insignificance, we tramped along the instep of the mountains. I walked second, but in reality more than at any other time alone. Here there was nobody to whom I might give something of myself.

"So lay yourself down in me," said the white cool silk.

The snow gradually increased, the valley narrowed. Sometimes one of us slipped and the cross-country ski poles strapped at the back of the backpacks struck each other. The snowshoes too clattered one against the other. Individual spruces massed into a spruce forest on the ever closer slopes.

From one side a dim, murmuring mountain stream approached.

"Would you have believed," I interrupted the lengthy silence, "that we could have got this far?" But in that moment something broke—the spell that despite all pain had brought me a liberating feeling of completion evaporated with finality and there remained only the bitter knowledge that I was escaping. And what was more: that this escape and the whole story had been planned by someone else instead of me.

We walked on for some six hundred meters. A small wooden bridge carried us over to the other side, where the route vanished in a a bushy tunnel. I wiped a little piece of the balustrade. A ring of ice clasped the current of water from both sides. I glanced backward. The village was still glinting a little at the beginning of the plateau. "I wouldn't have said," I said, "that we had climbed so far." At that moment two cones of light separated themselves from the village and smoothly, ominously, glided in our direction. Something deep in me shuddered.

Tomas broke into a run. He ran and said nothing. I ran after him. The snow gave way and everything was churning at our backs. "We've got to turn off the road somewhere," I shouted in front of me.

He didn't answer.

I drew on all my strength, but the distance between us kept increasing. "But we don't have much time!"

"Here." He waited for me. To the right a strip perhaps a meter wide branched away. Without hesitation we veered off our course here. We ran through the undergrowth, crossed an empty space and began to climb through the wood, straight upward. The valley, the road, the stream were all gone. I was breathing like a machine. "What if he has the stronger will?" the question raced through my head. "What if he is altogether the stronger?" And it seemed to me that I couldn't keep up this tempo and that I would have to stop immediately. Nevertheless in the end it was he who stopped. We stood face to face and breathed wrenchingly. It was where the slope was breaking.

"We are raving mad," I forced the words out of myself.

"It's horrible," he nodded.

From both sides we were assailed by impenetrable darkness. And ahead the strip of path was ever less visible between the tree trunks.

"But tell me," I went on, still panting, "tell me what it was."

"I don't know; maybe nothing; maybe it's nonsense," He too was struggling for breath. "And now we won't find out—at least I hope not. But now we have to go."

We set off. It struck both of us that the car had probably already reached the tunnel below. That perhaps it had already passed it without interest. Or . . .

The tree trunks whipped past us furtively. Walking in the snow was laborious, slow. Now and then we missed the path and then painstakingly searched for it again. At other times we stood on one spot so long that we could hear the icy droplets striking our backpacks. Towns, streets, demolition-sites, stations . . . these were still traces of a civilization in which we had grown up. There we were capable of living even under a State of Emergency, in a time of want, oppression. Here in the forest no laws applied. Here it was a matter of indifference that we had foreign state documents around our necks. And if it was worth those people's while to chase us as far as here . . .

"It's ridiculous," said my skeptical "I." "Admit that it's ridiculous to believe they can be bothered with you at all."

"Maybe—maybe it's ridiculous," I said. "But those head-lamps looked as though they were aiming at us."

"Come off it! For what possible reason? What would it mean?"

The crowns of the spruces above my head swayed slightly.

"It's true," I anwered, "that something for which there is a reason usually has a meaning. But think how deep a meaning something must have when there isn't any reason for it."

Now I walked first. I counted my steps: one hundred, then two hundred, three hundred and fifty steps. The effort was coming as if from a distance—awful, but alien. "Come on, let's use the poles."

With relief we dropped everything. Tomas took off his hat and ran his hand through his sweat-soaked hair. I sensed him beside me, rather than seeing him.

I looked at my watch. It showed eleven. This meant we had been walking for three hours when I wouldn't have said we had been going for more than one. I realized that this forest made a perfect prison. Its edge—however near it might be—was for these moments unendingly withdrawn. We stood up to our knees in snow. The thought of digging ourselves in nagged at us persistently. But that would mean sleeping without a fire and so without water either.

I counted another three hundred steps. That made a total of six hundred and fifty. The forest was gradually changing in shape. Instead of bare trunks crowned with leaves the spruces growing here were covered from top to bottom with bushy branches and snow.

Six hundred and eighty steps. After eight hundred we

changed around. "We ought to dig ourselves in," said Tomas.

"Not yet, not for a moment," I almost shouted. Actually I couldn't imagine any such thing.

There was a gust of wind as we came out into clearer space. Thick frozen snow was now falling into our eyes. I bent down and put a piece of this white substance into my mouth to give my stomach the feeling that I was eating. But the feeling quickly passed and there remained an unquenchable longing for a nourishment without form or name. Anxiety seized me. I realized that to dig myself in in this state meant to freeze to death or to be seriously sick. At exactly the same moment I glimpsed, a little way beneath me, the silhouette of a wooden shelter.

IV

The tea we made over a fire of splinters from the floor had been drunk to the last irrecoverable drop. A draft ran through a hole in the roof and through cracks in the walls.

I closed the zipper and remained in the sleeping bag with nothing but her who had been lost since morning. "Where can she be now?" the thought struck me. "And is she even alive—my unhappy little girl? And if she lives, how does she feel when she thinks of me?"

The image was now so vivid that it seemed to me that we were here together. Then I remembered Mirela, and I was beyond words. But the picture of Livie surfaced again—this time a scene from the crowd—the last glimpse of her forehead, radiating a kindly yellow light. I huddled still deeper into my sleeping bag. As I lay in the middle of the wooden shack, which creaked in the wind and the unceasing snow, I was surrounded by a group of almost comically abashed wolves. The nearest one licked my face, and it stayed damp. His eyes were full of the pain that only a beast can feel when its Lord suffers. These eyes gazed at me prepared to bear the whole cross, if it was in the slightest degree possible. But it was not in the least possible, because the affliction of so exalted and at the same time so terrible a fate—to bear the cross—belonged to the Lord only. And so the wolf sank down on his front legs and trembled. "I know," I whispered and stretched out my hand to his muzzle. I could even have touched him, but despite his apparent devotion he didn't seem at all tame, only as if accidentally affected by the force of human misfortune. The other wolves were circling around us in ever smaller circles. "How terrible my situation must be," I thought, "if even wild beasts can feel it." But I was immediately assailed by a guilty sense that I was feeling sorry for myself instead of others.

"Leave it alone, you can't change anything anyway," I said.

And they did indeed withdraw, and only the most devoted wolf stayed and kept on trembling in the vacated space. He was not mourning now for me, but for the professor and his daughter Livie. This drew me to him in a sudden drift of warmth. I overcame my shyness and placed my hand on the back of his head. I stroked it with short movements up and down. He half-closed his eyes into narrow slits and they burned with suppressed wildness. I felt how tremendously his heart fought with the forbidden pleasure and at the same time submitted to it. But then he anxiously arched away, leaped . . . and was gone.

I remained in the landscape alone. The gray-white walls of the route reminded me of linen. And all my feelings, griefs, and guilts flowed together into one great gray-white feeling. I couldn't see the wolves, although they must have been there. On a branch jutting out into the route sat Tomas and he preached these words: "It is hard, when someone loses somebody—really hard, I know. When you consider that a person has only one life . . . " It struck me that this meant absolutely nothing. It was distasteful to listen to him and a nuisance to go around him. "Don't bother your head with it, " I said. "It won't be you who falls down that slope, but me."

I continued on, for a moment satisfied with myself. It gave me courage to see my life from a greater distance. Prague. What was really left to me of the city when I looked back? An occasional sense of home, a few written lines, a little bitterness, a little hatred, a couple of summer evenings. And I had abandoned it for a short while, thirsting for a change, but in the fundamental belief that all was as it should be with me. And in the town in the foothills of this Country, where I had wanted to spend a few hours on a journey lasting no more than a few days, I meet her: my wild, inevitable, fine, deep complement—so irrevocable, that I don't hesitate to tell Tomas, just in conversation: "She is a part of me." Now, as I realized how indissoluble this union was, I felt as if I had driven a wedge into myself. It was no longer the soft image of Livie transforming itself in gestures and forms: In my own body I found pieces of flesh belonging to her. I grasped that if I returned, this flesh would begin to disintegrate; it would be totally spoiled. What would follow would be the rotting and falling away of entire slices of myself. The process of adaptation.

The landscape divided and differentiated itself on both sides. Condensed forms betrayed the presence of wolves. It was possible to make out a stool, and two pairs of girl's shoes. At the corner a girl appeared. At first I could only see her legs and as I drew closer the joy of reunion rose up in me. But instead of Livie it was suddenly Martina: the Martina whose image had been recalled by someone in the train corridor, and whom they would have depicted, in a prehistoric age, as a goddess and mother of the race. She stood five meters away, facing me, and she was naked. At first I was taken aback by this substitution, but then I began to perceive the challenge in her apparition. At her side stood a wolf, its fur touching her hips. Awareness of that touch was arousing. Involuntarily I imagined her having intercourse with a pack of wolves. Her raven hair fell from her sparkling forehead.

I opened my eyes and slid my head out of the sleeping bag. But in the icy room there was no trace of Martina. Yet only a moment ago she had almost been mine. I now didn't know if I should rejoice because she could have belonged to me or because she had left and I remained faithful to Livie.

I pulled my head back in. The inside of the sleeping bag was cold along the zipper. The chill attacked from all sides; the warm place remaining was insignificant. "These night quarters," it struck me, "solve nothing. In the morning we shall have to set off again . . . . And these inexhaustible masses of snow: myself on the inside and everywhere nothing but snow."

I couldn't believe that the image of Martina had really been lost. I tried in vain to keep hold of the vision of her hips. "First Livie," I thought, "and now Martina."

I reached the very edge of the landscape. Muddy clusters turned into houses. Streets full of houses. Suddenly there was One Thousand and Twenty-Three—the Cudeans' house. Its walls still pointed upward, calm and inviolate. But the ground beneath them was already hollow. A shot rang out. The building shook in a brief convulsion; it folded like a curtain; for a moment everything was enveloped in smoke. When it cleared, instead of the house there was only a yawning hole. The street swam in a flood of white rays. The sidewalk too grew lighter and seemed perfectly prepared. On the opposite side a little girl and a man were playing. A beautiful little girl, a high-spirited young man. "Who is it?"

"It is Livie—Livie Cudean. And that man is her father. Simeonu Cudean."

V

In the clearing between the door and the forest the breeze had blown the fallen snow over the tops of the tree stumps.

The sleeping bag was covered with thin slivers of frost. It was the first mountain day.

Tomas appeared at the door with a mess-tin. "Not a footprint left," he burst out. "This is what I call a morning in the mountains."

Pitilessly I tore at the zipper. Then I gazed as if on a miracle at this suddenly guileless piece of nature under its cloudy cape. The ridge sloped slightly upward, and so where the clearing ended I could only see the bottoms of the trees. The morning frost whipped into my eyes. Where had they gone, insecurity, concealment, secrecy? Perhaps their traces had also been snowed over. There remained simply "being" in a sparkling prison. And the unmistakable feeling that this was not a propitious place to live.

"Tomas," I said at breakfast, "do you think I ought to have done more for her?"

"You couldn't do anything." He fell silent and then launched out: "What do you think was the meaning of the car?"

I quickly considered what it was he was getting at: If I denied the existence of a threat there would be no reason to go on. And if I admitted it . . . "Well, I think," I started, "that whatever it meant, we can't be certain that they aren't following us. You were running yourself, after all."

"So you want to keep going on up!"

For a moment I hesitated. "Yeah."

"Okay," he said, as if it didn't concern him. Vexed, I fastened my snowshoes to my feet. We proceeded toward the ridge, gloomy and stooping. The snowshoes sank into loose snow unwilling to release them.

"I'd like to see where you'll get this way," smirked my skeptical "I." "If you at least had some kind of goal."

The going was awful. But Tomas's step was calm—almost too calm. I dashed up to his level and on my left I had his indifferent face. "It's impossible this way," I shouted, "You can't pretend that you're fulfilling my wish."

He stopped and looked me in the eye. "But Martin, this is your game. I'm not looking for anything important here. What happened is terrible, I admit it. But at home I've got Irena waiting for me. And the prospect of being a surgeon there. So if you want to achieve something in this Country, that's just your business, I have no interest in it."

His certainty was crushing. He must have thinking it over a long time if he could speak so harshly, but so calmly.

"I don't know," he added appeasingly, "maybe you remember why we came here in the first place. Here we've got mountains, snow; we have everything here, don't we? Let's walk over the ridges and go home."

I didn't know whether I was supposed to fall down on the ground or pull myself together and leave. No, there was no sense in putting into words what could only be made up for by an act of which I was not capable: the act of acceptance or the act of destruction. And at that moment—without my causing it—words were wrenched to my lips: "Lord, I accept." But even these I did not utter and a bottomless solitude swelled in my entrails.

The silence of the virgin forest in the high mountains spread itself out. Someone's tracks led across the path. A fox? A lynx? "What must it be like," I thought, "to be born here and never, never go down."

The trees were becoming smaller and more sparse. The forest, until now unmarked by human footsteps, was gradually shifting. But when it gets late and the mounds of snow remain as endless as the sea, what shall I do then? I eased the straps from my shoulders, took off my gloves, and clasped the handle of my stick with my warmed palm. "Tomas, there's no point in going on."

His face showed surprise: "You don't want to go any further?" I got the impression he was making fun of me. "We simply have nowhere to go," I whispered, devoid of will.

"And so you want to go back the same way?"

I merely shrugged my shoulders. Ever since he had told me what he thought, I had been feeling strangely guilty, subdued.

"And what if we went directly down the slope?" he suggested after a while. In vain I tried to guess what he was really thinking.

So we unstrap our snowshoes and slide down the snow-clogged gully. "You treat life like a well-stocked table," I think. "You add a little vinegar here, a bit more salt there, a touch more pepper. You take a couple of spoonfuls of understanding and a couple of spoonfuls of morality and mix them with the question of the meaning of being. But you always have the option of getting up from the table and leaving."

We lose altitude quickly; we are surrounded by almost impenetrable undergrowth. We get around it along the edges of boulders. My foot slips and I fall into branches. One arm is bruised, something snaps. I am lying among branches, snow down my neck: above me the loneliness of the forest prison. "Just don't rate yourself too highly," my skeptical "I" sneers triumphantly. "After all you yourself do nothing but speculate, consider, calculate. Maybe more than him."

"Yes," I reply, still flat on my back. "I calculate with each step. But in the flow of time I surrender myself."

A strange twilight has settled in the treetops—some kind of sun the color of black-gray. Black-gray rays penetrate through the branches; and the tragedy, not so much of the following hours as of the following days, makes its presence felt in the world of the forest. And I can see, without being able to influence anything, the hopeless fatefulness with which our path is running into it. And not only this path— our whole journey from its first minutes at the Prague station, from the clatter of the wheels carrying us through the holy night, from the no-man's-land surrounded by a wreath of wires, from our meeting with the Cudean family. But this is all long past; nothing remains but to look ahead—for a few more days.

"Yes indeed," snivels an ancient tree stump, "it's not a time for a happy life. Let's look up together, where the black sun is rising."

We are descending as before. An ever warmer breeze blows from the valley. "I would never have believed," I say half to myself, "how easily the weather changes here." The skin on my forehead and hands is burning.

Finally it has become possible to run down the soapy film, which becomes thinner and thinner. Another few hundred meters and the road is here. On the road there are some completely melted patches. How safe it feels to stand on one of them. And what a fall for someone who wanted to aim for the peaks. The valley here is narrow, constricted. A little way up, a still narrower valley opens into it. In the moist crotch of the mountains stands a hut. When I catch sight of it, at first I freeze. Into my mind leaps the Restaurant Europa. Arching high above the hut are rocky ravines covered in ice, where balls of cloud are rolling.

We are coming up toward the crossroads. A wooden foot-bridge leads toward us from the log hut. Seen close up everything is disproportionately large.

"Do you want to go in?" I ask.

"Yes I do," he replies.

We walk across the bridge. What we have in front of us is indeed a mountain hut, perhaps with accommodation. Over the battered door the proud inscription: "Cafenea." There is a stale smell, entirely familiar. Once again I look around— perhaps to discover a black car, which could easily be hidden in the bushes nearby. We enter the door. Out of the dimness loom lumberjack faces above an army of unfinished bottles. Uncertainly we proceed toward an empty table. I catch several glances. We slide onto the bench still with our heavy backpacks. Somebody gets up, sways, tries to give us a bottle and a hand. At this moment he stumbles, and hits the table-top with his belly. A geyser of vomit gushes and gushes.

VI

Drunken, warm, stinking waves of forgetfulness. Long ago dried out; only sometimes my hand wanders to the crust on my trousers. The landscape behind the small window sinks into twilight.

The lumberjack who vomited at the beginning now finally took his paw off my shoulder and embraced Tomas. "Prostie," he repeats at least five times. Shots of liquor are entering his mouth as into a large black pit. We just nod our heads. "Prostie." "Prostie," I hear myself say against a background of increasing hubbub. The lumberjack and Tomas are drawing apart; they spin together with the room. Our story has an interval; it has lain down at the threshold. If we got up, its ears would prick up and its hairs rise. But since we sit, it sleeps. We are free. When shall we be so lucky again?

When I looked at my watch, it was five and behind the window was darkness. The woman dispensing alcohol stood indifferently at a bar that resembled a coffin-lid—it was so cold. Everywhere worn-out faces with the unmistakable trace of grief.

"You've got us again," I hissed at the hazy vision of this female figure who mediated the relationship between the forest workers and a liquid state-supported heaven. She irritated me. (She stood on the banks of gaiety, just as I did.)

"So what do you want!?" I turned toward her again. "Do you want us to roll here on the cold piss-covered floor? And when that happens, will you make the sign of the cross over us or simply turn off the lights because your working hours are over?"

I laid my head on the tabletop and felt the need to return to my story. To walk out of the bar and look it in the eyes. Although I knew that if I did, it would be like flinging myself into a river above wild rapids ending in a waterfall. For the time being I could at least gaze past the window glass into the spreading night.

The rapidly ended past merged there with the future. At the very limit stood a lichen-covered spruce—the tree that had sprung from my hand. We two were once again linked bodily. And it was as if my hand remembered its dance from the train. It detached itself from me; it could not be kept back. With crooked fingers it pointed forward and then back. It thrashed in the mud and snowdrifts. It ran down the town streets. It jumped onto a pale blue table surrounded by a yellow kitchen. It drew a red heart. It added a shovel sharp as an arrow. It traced the heart. The springs of blood gushed.

"I really should go out to the threshold," I thought, and immediately imagined the bitter mountain air and indigestible eternity of the universe that would strike me there.

But I went nowhere. From behind the horizon I could scent, even where I sat, that strange spruce. It grew through my chest.

"We could eat here," murmured Tomas and pulled out some cheese.

"Take out the bread as well," I said and I was almost scared that my voice too was so hasty and hollow. "And offer the lumberjack something."

But the lumberjack turned his head away, afraid. I tried to read his Tartar face to find out if he was young. He stared at the food with pretended indifference. Once again I made the offer with my eyes, and he staggered sadly away across the room.

"What happened?" asked Tomas.

I shrugged. I felt somehow guilty. At that moment Livie could hold back no longer and took my head in her arms.

"Don't worry about it," she said, "the people here are like that." I could feel her warmth flowing into my temples.

"Come off it," I looked sadly up at her. "It's my fault— without you I'm not good enough. And I abandoned you, my dearest girl."

"Abandoned? . . . You held on to me as long as you could. Even now I can still feel you clasping my hand."

"You don't have to placate me needlessly," I said softly. "I know that it's my fault, even though we were powerless. You pushed on further and further—you had to be in the center of events. And I couldn't prevent it. I couldn't prevent it because I loved you for it."

I sat, she stood, I freed my head from her embrace and caressed her palm. "Livie," it struck me suddenly. "Are you still alive?"

She was silent.

"And your father?"

She clenched her fingers and tears of helplessness welled up in her eyes. "They used batons against us."

"So you see. Could my guilt be greater?"

"It could. If you had abandoned me. But you will not abandon me."

Once again she shone with sweet delight: "We'll be together forever—just think, what happiness."

"Only," I stopped, suddenly alarmed. "Only I am here. God knows, I'll have you inside myself. . . . Or do you have something more in mind?"

"What I have in mind is our complete union."

I stroked the bony ridge of her hand. She smiled from behind the smoke and creeping stench, but relief no longer flowed toward me. And she stood—a flame of light—a paradise of eternal closeness promised in a mist. At this moment someone forgot to close the door; Livie seemed to be extinguished; a raw wind blew through the room. Some ten heads turned toward the crack of the door. Darkness yawned there—insolent and naked, the wind was breaking between the door hinges—blowing from occupied towns and deepening snowfields, from the Country of martial law, lead, and batons, from the land of hope and ruin, longing and discovery. It hurtled over trodden-down splinters of ice. It struck against the creaking doorframe.

VII

At first it seemed to me that left and right rose Prague—gigantic, touching the heavens, with the brave curve of the Castle. Then the rooftops vanished, leaving a vast gloomy throne prepared for the Last Judgment. Quickly and surely we climbed along its pedestal toward the heights. I had heartburn, my arteries thumped, effort gushed from my mouth like something that had nothing to do with me. The freezing snow cracked under my feet.

Deep and long sounded the trumpets. On a slope above us several trees broke into flame; the fire engulfed the spreading branches. The top of a rocky pillar flowed with subdued light. There stood Romu astride, and his shadow (as if the light came from a single source) fell toward us. In the background was an illuminated house, with a facade that I knew intimately. The soft light gave it an added charm that belongs elsewhere to the solitude of churches. But then, without Romu raising a hand, there happened what had already happened once—the walls began to crumble and everything vanished, but before the fall I recalled the candlestick, the tin radio, the attic, the room, and the yellow kitchen. And it was strange to watch a place where one person had loved another disappearing from the world.

The collapse ended, but Romu still stood on the rocky pillar, and the wolves—like his blood brothers—stood on smaller towers. They were all truly like brothers. "And I had the impression," I looked up, "that you were not kin to his blood but to mine. What should I think of your message now? How should I now understand the way you came to the town gates and let my face merge with your fur? What of your aiming for the distance and your floating? What of the compassion that you gave me? Are you listening?"

But instead of answer there was only the cracking of burned branches. High above, the animal silhouettes were set in motion; I saw them emerging from behind protruding shapes, and then vanishing again. More and more trees were bursting into flame near us, and so our path led through a labyrinth of snow and fire. We walked forward fast, shoulder to shoulder. "Tomas," I called to my companion, but it was clear that between us there was a severing of all links.

We crossed a stream. Romu left his place on the summit and broke into a run. A second trumpet sounded, deeper and longer than the first. The floodgates of turbid waters opened and a mixture like concrete poured down beneath us into the landscape of the valley. I realized that Romu was only the executor of a higher will. I was still very drunk. But even so I saw the streambed and the whole ravine filling up. Fire had already caught on several bushes, coals flew through the air, and there was a hissing. It was clear that the wolves and perhaps even Romu were getting close. Then the third trumpet sounded and this was the order established: the first trumpet came up from the womb of the universe that ends nowhere, deep, long, and urgent, and it resembled an annunciation; the second trumpet came up from the darkness that enwraps everything, still deeper, still longer and yet more urgent, and it resembled a rumbling; but this third came up from the womb of matter, into which everything returns, the deepest, the longest, the most urgent, and it was like an earthquake. Several trees ripped up from their roots. In the sky the stars trembled, glittering from behind the clouds.

We came to the first fallen tree, climbed up, and jumped into the unviolated snow. I turned around and was immediately surprised by the overabundance of red light pouring from the valley. From the roots came the scent of loosened earth. It occurred to me that we were too secluded here. As if to confirm this thought, a four-legged animal pattered around us and smacked its lips. Against all logic I imagined that I was at home in my room. I am standing by the bed and objects do not speak. But this lasts only a moment and I am back again: I, Tomas, the animal; behind our backs the devastation of the valley. The jaws and eyes of the wolves draw nearer. There will be no more trumpets. Only the sharp sound of a whistle giving the order for destruction.

"It is too late for anything," is the only thought that strikes me. I see Tomas tottering beside me. The snow disappears, the ground gives way; we are falling forever into its depths and hell is opening. I think of everyone and no one, of home, of the world. But home and the world are hopelessly escaping. I too am escaping. Into a space that is not. In violation of the laws of this instant I am caught by someone's hand. A real human hand. I look up and, to my surprise, see Remu's shining face.

REMU

I

WHEN I WOKE UP THIS REMARKABLE PERSON WAS STILL asleep. Foamy saliva trickled down his beard and there was a sound of snoring. Somber rays of light fell down into the cave from several illuminated spots. In contrast to the tension that had reigned this morning, Remu's lack of constraint was a promise of safety. "While he is here," I thought, "nothing bad can happen." Again and again I was compelled to look at his powerful blanket-wrapped body. At one point he moved, reminding me of a sleeping saurian or an ancient Greek god resting in the heart of Olympus. It was he who had caught me last night before I plunged into the rocky gulley. I could still feel his hand on my shoulder.

I dragged myself a little way into the icy air. Tomas was also already up. From outside something fateful was approaching—something more than just the arbitrary power of the police. And there was no doubt that these reflected rays of light were the carriers of this fatefulfulness.

Remu now turned over onto his side and stopped snoring. Thomas whispered something into the sudden silence. Although he was speaking quite audibly, I couldn't understand a single word. "What?"

He did not react.

I repeated more sharply: "What?!"

Helplessly he regarded me from the sleeping bag in which he sat propped against the wall of the cave.

Words then started to gush indifferently from his mouth. This time I could hear entirely clearly, but no message penetrated to me. "I don't understand you at all," I thought. "You are speaking a hostile, somehow foreign, language."

After a while Remu too woke up. His brown eyes, as soon as they opened, were full of a paternal and comradely smile. "How can he smile," I sighed, "on so strange a morning?" Immediately I felt a longing to say something to him in my native language. It was the same longing that used to grip me when I was talking with Livie. But Remu had already got up and in the dim light even his gaiety seemed rather uncertain—hiding a thorn of pain. He threw the blanket into his pack and nodded upward. We packed quickly—I and some companion of mine (I could not remember his name or where I had acquired him). He was throwing the remaining things into a large blue backpack.

Remu was ready first. He stuck a pipe between his lips, and a flat beret on his head. He was winking at me as if we had just met. All the while he gesticulated appreciatively, referring to all the long past days. It struck me that nothing is so easily recognizable as the grief of a robust man: the mountain of muscles sinks, strength begins to ebb purposelessly from the body.

We came out of the cave above a landscape full of snow. I looked first downward to the mouth of the valley and then higher between the burned spruce tops, and finally to the transparent sky, at the edge of which stood the source of all tension: the black, shining coal disk of the sun. Shining rays poured from it in a stream of precious stones and most of these missed the earth's surface. The few that fell on the rocks, on us, and on the frozen snow brought anxiety and chill. Remu first clenched his jaws under his beard and only then started walking. He went first, after him the one with the blue backpack and after him, I myself. We traversed the steep slope above the side gulley. I noticed trampled patches that here reached the very edge. At my heart I felt short, rapid shudders.

We surmounted the dangerous area and climbed through a series of ever smaller trees. The mountain air was sharp; it tasted rare. I became aware of the landscape around me changing beyond recall: the snow had become more powdery, the trees more enveloped, with branches reaching down to the ground. There was no doubt that the unearthly world of the plains was already drawing close.

"I don't know," my skeptical "I" whispered after a long time, "maybe you ought to stop and embrace these stones! Stop and press yourself to their skin—the wrinkled fruit of the earth. And she will give you the strength to go home to everyday human destinies!"

But I said: "No. You can't want me to touch these untouchable trees." At this my skeptical "I" climbed out of my head and pulled itself toward the nearest tree. "At least ask Remu where he's taking you! He's a simple man—he has nothing to conceal," it called.

A little puzzled I looked into the piercing eyes of this other self. The eyes reproached and at the same time begged. "What are you doing?" I forced myself to stutter placatingly. "You'll freeze to death here." But already the gap between myself and my companions had widened to several dozen paces. Despite the continuing reproach I broke into a run.

"I shan't freeze to death," declared my skeptical "I," now from somewhere above me, "I shall wander through these forests like an eternal question mark over the meaning of your story."

Remu kept on striding ahead. While the distressing rays of light slipped into the forest through the spider's web of branches, I mentally told him the whole story of myself and Livie. Yes, I wanted to ask him where he lived, if he had a wife, how he made a living. "And reading," it occurred to me, "did he know how to read?"

Hunger and complete exhaustion set my head spinning. It was only with difficulty that I kept going, despite the fact that a path had already been trodden. Remu stopped and pulled out his flask. A whiff of his stale breath floated round my lips. I caught the searching look he fixed on the path behind us. "Fratele meu,"* he said, and pointed down. I looked in that direction and he knit his brow as if he knew he could not ward off danger. "Fratele meu."

I saw our still single track and I had an inkling that some deep connection between himself and our pursuers lay in his words. I remembered all those unpleasant bailiffs—Lanky, Romu, the chief with the cat face. What I felt was not hatred or fear, but desolation—the boundless desolation of their ruined lives. "In my country it's the same," I said in Czech. "I think these people are estranged even from themselves."

My knees were touching the powdery snow. Around us were spruces mixed with dwarf pines and everything was drawing away into the distance, first in a mild and then a sharper slope. To the left towered a great rounded mountain, protecting us from the sun—that overflowing wound of the night.

"So we've had a good chat," gestured Remu and returned the flask to his pack. At that moment I wasn't sure whether I could go on at all. If somebody had said: "Lie down here, Martin," my wish would have been fulfilled. But from above came only silence.

We found ourselves at the foot of a precipice. By now only small tufts of dwarf-pine made little humps in the dunes. Beyond rose the uninterrupted realm of snow. My companions went on while I stood still. Incapable of words I gazed at their slow, rhythmic efforts. Always first trod Remu, and behind him with the blue backpack, . . . who was that other figure really? He had snowshoes tied to his

*"My brother."

pack as I did. He had cross-country poles in his hands just as I did. He was somehow very close to me and somehow even more alien. As if he had been blown here by my half-awakened mind from another life preceding my birth.

The gap widened and seemed to be a chasm, but I kept standing. A deadly cold was flowing down the slope. I knew that I had to put at least a little food in my stomach. I dropped my pack from my shoulders and at the same moment realized that I had a little food in my pocket. It did indeed contain a slice of salami and a few squares of chocolate. I put the chocolate into my paralyzed mouth.

Remu now noticed my delay and hurried down. He ran right up to me: "Dificultate? Problema?"

"No, it's all right now," my eyes whispered to his.

He vigorously gestured at my pack.

"No, it's not necessary," I smiled. "It's really not necessary now." I felt the chocolate in my stomach doing its job.

He bounced his own pack up and down to show how light it was.

"I know," I nodded, "I know it's light. But it's hard to go first, . . . first." I pointed at the untrodden snow.

Then he looked questioningly at my feet, to see if they were the cause of my lagging.

"Well, I'll admit it. But it's really all right now." I began to feel exhausted by the talk. He looked at me helplessly, the beret sitting casually on his head and under it a hood over his ears, in his worn-out coat he was ready to offer any kind of help.

I hoisted my pack on my back and we set off. Or more accurately, we crawled on all fours, the slope was so steep. We climbed right up to the place where the third was waiting. Gradually I stopped thinking of the physical effort and devoted myself to thoughts of the approaching highest point, relief and reconciliation.

Then the horizon opened and Remu took off his cap.

The tops of the hills ran pacifically to the edge of this

mountain kingdom. The black rays flowed round them and poured a deep self-pity into our hearts. In the world there is no sin greater than to stand idle in the moment of vision.

"Ech," exhaled Remu.

"Yes," said I.

The third uttered something incomprehensible.

We started out across the spreading plain. The surface of the snow was hard here, and so we didn't sink into it. We could walk alongside each other without the least difficulty. The sun—the cup of bitterness set above us—leaned on my back and slightly warmed it. The tops of the mountains created a great cauldron, at the same time resembling a cup. From the depths of the cauldron crept a gray-white ocean of haze, threatening to overflow into the blue vault of heaven.

"So I'm in the mountains now," I thought. "Isn't that by any chance what I once wanted?" But below, hidden in mist, waited naked reality and we were already dropping down. Remu looked at his timepiece, apparently uneasy. "How far does he want to go, for God's sake? Why doesn't he stop for a moment? What are we lacking here?" And immediately I answered myself: "It's her. She is lacking here." While we had been climbing, it had all seemed to have some foundation. But now we were already descending. Most of all I would have liked to lie down on the spot. Remu somehow sensed this and looked over his shoulder apologetically, with a glance that said "Have faith!"

The plateau narrowed; we were now walking along a broad extensive ridge. I on the right, Remu in the middle. On the left the third. His backpack, snowshoes, poles disquieted me. He seemed to be very persistent. When it was clear which way we were going, he even walked dozens of meters ahead. Sometimes he tried to say something in an incomprehensible language. At other times we trod on alongside each other silently.

We came to a saddle between two mountains. The ever

darker disk of the sun had already slipped down to the edge and was ready to abandon the afternoon sky. Horizontal rays blended strangely with the white snow.

Remu stopped; I found myself facing him. We looked at each other. "Well, say something," I thought. "But let it be understandable. Or take out the flask." But he stood and spoke in the most eloquent of all languages. Then he took up his stick and sketched a house.

The house lay between us. I looked at the drawing dully, without emotion. "A house. So what?"

Remu pointed at the house, and then at himself, and waved his stick downward. He was already setting off in that direction. As he bent, black rays ran through his throat and hand.

And I—as I stepped in the same direction—trod on the window of the house. There was a terrifying crashing, clanging, and laughter. I was suffused with heat and the crashing didn't stop. It seemed that the whole universe wanted to use the opportunity to spit on me.

"Soon now it will be New Year's Eve," the thought struck me like a reaction to the still resounding laughter. "If I wanted, I could go home for the New Year." The word depressed and warmed: "Home. But if she is lost, I simply can't.

"Livie Cudean, that strange girl, lost. I can't even precisely recall her face. How did you manage it, Livie Cudean, growing into me?" But as soon as the thought came to me, her nearness was again embodied. Bodily, warm, smooth girl's skin, emanating a glow. I felt aimless, and I knew that the way to the glow led not to home but into the womb of this Country.

As soon as we had descended from the ridge our legs started to sink in the piled-up snow. I had stopped expecting such trouble: we sank knee-deep in snow, my backpack was tying me down, the straps digging into my collarbone and shoulders. I was starting to shake with rage. "Damned journey! Damned Remu! Damned snow!" I would probably have flung my pack to the ground, if beside me, on the unmarked plateau, I hadn't noticed an animal's track. Clear, springy, lonely, it stretched into eternity and held a scrap of destiny. I gazed with it, and with an awakened sense of my own direction, back toward the ridge. There the track ribbon vanished and again emerged until it dissolved in the misty dimness—a dimness advancing unstoppably above the white, starry sky that looked like a desert.

Oh yes, an awakened sense of direction. I freed, reconciled, and delivered myself. I saw it above myself, found it in myself and adhered to it. I put rage aside forever and trod on in a humility breached only by that third, whose backpack shone here like an indecipherable but insistent reminder of other possibilities and other directions. I was kicked in the face by the mounting frost and Remu pointed: "Down! Come down as quickly as possible!"

"What are you thinking about?" The question came after a while from some consciousness previously unknown to me.

"Well," I answered, "it occurred to me that if there was a television standing somewhere in this snow, and broadcasting, I would have no idea what sort of miracle it was—that picture in it. Like a dumb simpleton I would look and say: Batteries? Resistors? Waves? And if the picture then went out, the television would become a useless box enveloped in silence."

"That is correct reasoning," nodded the consciousness silently.

"And if, for instance, my jacket fell apart or my watch broke down," I continued, encouraged, "I would be just as helpless. I don't, you see, know anything at all—I, a human being—about the nature of man's inventions. When I think about it, I feel as if . . . as if borrowed."

The sun was setting and the tragic event that it revealed drew close. Not far below, the silhouettes of forests already appeared. On the opposite slope shone a building.

"Bravo!" shouted Remu with his right hand raised high. "Bravo!" And he jumped on one leg. Immediately he was joined by the third traveler. They were slapping each other and squeezing each other's hands. They were dancing. Meanwhile a small black halo drifted up and enveloped Remu's head. But the two were unstoppable. I stood beside them wordless.

It took a whole eternity before we descended to the bottom of the glen. From under the ice bubbled water. Remu led us up to a board and a wooden weir. The stream rolled here from the heights and roared into the darkness that had already fallen. Carefully we crossed over. From below us the cold blew as from the grave.

On the other side a well-trodden path began. I crossed last and, stopping to tie my bootlace, I stayed in the glen alone. But between the stream and the slope stood a great candlestick sunk to its shoulders in the snow. As if bewitched I stared at its ninefold arms. "What are you doing here?" I forced the words from myself.

"What should I be doing? I'm growing."

"Growing?"

"Yes, growing. From the copper hidden in the earth."

It really did look now as if the waste was the field and the candlestick its fruit.

"Perhaps you might know," it occurred to me after a while. "Remu, the one who passed here a moment ago, he had around his head a small black radiance."

But the candlestick was silent.

"Such a small black radiance."

Again nothing.

"I wondered," I tried once more, "whether this might not mean . . . I admit that I probably shouldn't ask, but . . . "

Both my companions had definitely left. But I had no reason to hurry. Only the last precipice separated me from the end of my journey.

"And what about Mirela? What about down there?"

The silence thickened with only the falling water murmuring into it from one side. The candlestick imperceptibly glistened. I laid aside my backpack and poles; then my gloves and hat. I took one step. The candlestick relented and seemed silently to laugh. There was only myself and it. I clasped my hands.

II

I went up the trodden trail all alone. A few stars glittered in the otherwise cloudy sky and somewhere behind the mountains the moon was preparing to rise. At last the silhouette of a building appeared above me. In its single small window flickered the reflection of a fire. At that moment I slowed down. The trail wound sharply upward. I realized that my companions had long been sitting down. That they had long been warm and long been drinking tea. It was only I who was out here, still tormenting myself.

At last I reach the tramped threshold. Leaning on the door stands Remu, gazing happily above the wide, wide landscape. "Good evening," I say. "Buna," he replies. The chalet is built entirely of wood and set into the slope with its back growing out from the hillside. It is full of cracks, not a single tightly fitting beam. Remu opens the door. The first thing I see is a fire and boiling water. I step on the trampled earth and something startles me. But yes, everything is disproportionately larger. It has an animal-shed smell and at the back, the back behind a barrier, a small herd of sheep is pressed together. By the walls, heaps of fodder; an inexhaustible supply of wood. The whole chalet is really half a cave. But the presence of the sheep creates an atmosphere of home. At last I see people as well: on a bench by the fire sits the third, and behind him in the corner. . . . Is it possible? Is it really Martina? This girl has long black hair and a clear forehead. . . . Yes, it is she. Only the expression on her face is unusually relaxed, rid of all striving. The only object of her interest remains, even after my arrival, a wooden cradle. From inside the cradle comes a mewling.

I feel Remu's hand on my back. "I know, I can take off my backpack. I know." I take down the pack and Remu urges me again. "I know, I can come in." I take these few paces and once again something mewls. I look at Martina and then over the rim of cradle at two tiny wolfcubs huddling there. I look again at Martina and now she returns my glance. With not a hint of remembrance, no will to draw nearer to me. Remu comes up close beside her. He looks tired and content. I look alternately at the wolfcubs and at these two. Remu puts his hand on her shoulder, very tenderly, more like a protector than a man. I nod my head and smile. The wolfcubs in the cradle make contented purring noises.

I sit down by the fire and from that moment I am totally finished. I ought to eat but I haven't the strength. I can't even make up my mind to untie my boots. I look indifferently into the yellow-red flames. Remu frisks about; he scatters a fistful of chicory into the cauldron. As time passes, the chalet and everything in it begins to seem to me like a strange consoling dream. I can hear the moving bodies of the sheep. Behind the barrier there is even a trough and water trickles through it. The banked-up logs crack. But it is December, it is winter. It is a State of Emergency and the mountain plateaus are fatal. The road we took out there separates us from the inhospitable world.

At last I take off my boots. On each heel I have a large red patch. My soles resemble cottage cheese. My eyes search for Martina, to see if she will at least notice me now. But Martina is giving suck. In the flickering light I see a wolfcub and a long white breast. Martina is standing calm and grave, holding to herself a small wolf body and head. If I want, I can see the other breast as well, swelling out at the edge of a woolen bedspread. Chastely I avert my sight. It is hard not to think of Livie as I gaze into the waving flames. Even though, understandably, Livie is other than Martina is now. Livie is a young girl and Martina in her motherhood is so enchanting that all memories of the time when I knew her seem out of place and absurd. But Livie has in her body everything necessary for her to be, someday, in Martina's place.

Remu pours the chicory mixture into half-rusted mugs. He wants to inspect my feet. I try to stop him; I stretch out my arm and at that moment accidentally touch his beard. In surprise he looks at me; for an instant we are both embarrassed and I see his brown, attention-catching eyes. They resemble fertile land.

I am sipping chicory from the tin mug, which warms. Drinking here like me is the third, too. I scan his sportsman's body with mild distaste. How come he is with us, even here? Neither the expression on his face nor his blond hair suits this place. Despite this I have the feeling that his presence here somehow concerns me. That it aims toward something outside these wooden beams.

"Above all, no enmity," it was a reprimand from the consciousness springing from within me. "Better rest your gaze in the depths of this dully illuminated room. That way you will understand that even your own journeying, although here you have reached the very edge, only aims somewhere through this place."

"But these are two quite different things," I object. "Mine—and here you are probably right—aims. But his? He is like a fetter pulling toward the earth. Like a shutter placed between me and this calming world." I myself am surprised by this thought. I have the feeling that I have uncovered the reason why he bothers me. "But," I add, "you are right that I ought to be patient with him."

The wind hits the door, the fire flares up more strongly. Once again we strangely fail to engage, I and he. One of the wolfcubs squeaks, behind the barrier several sheep are bleating. The blond head of my companion turns in curiosity.

Later we sit all four around the glowing stones. I have partly changed my clothes, and even eaten some soup. I want to sleep. But whenever I close my eyes, images of the mountains flash across my retina. Martina is sitting between me and Remu, beside her the cradle, and she notices none of us people. Remu, without thought of gratitude, guards her. When I give him a comprehending look, he shrugs his shoulders and smiles conspiratorially. Suddenly I wonder who has been looking after Martina in the last two days. Or the time when Remu was traveling from the border on an international train. "Why should you ask who takes care of the flower that grows on the rock?" interposes my springing consciousness. "Nourished from the stone, the wind, sun and rain, . . . and yet: does this suffice for her to live? And who takes care of the wind, so that it blows, and of the rain which falls life-givingly? You have reached as far as the common foundation, for you will not discover the principle by which the inanimate is quickened." I gaze at that once intelligent but now only blissful face of Martina—mother of four-legged little creatures—and I have the feeling that there is a word growing in me which . . . once again I look at her fair face . . . yes, the word is "grace" and is a gift of that force through which she survives.

Quietly I rise and walk across the cold clay. In my heart I try to resurrect the image of a thin girl, muffled in a sleeping bag. But instead of the picture there are only colors, brush-strokes, a palate of lips. "This is how it is then. She has dissolved in me, she has become a pure principle, an idea. All that remains to me is a trail that aims toward her inside me. But she herself has departed from the human garment."

For a moment I stop at the wooden barrier. The reflection of the flames falls even here and illuminates the bodies of the sheep. Involuntarily I count: one, two, three . . . nine. Nine sheep. I warm my hands on their shaggy bodies.

I go back to the fire. But suddenly everyone rises and prepares for sleep. "But after all . . . !" I have a feeling that if we don't sleep now, something fateful will change. But the space is already empty. The flames whip into a darkness resembling the prematurely forsaken womb of a woman. "Perhaps we have just wasted everything," I think. "Perhaps we have just lost everything. Perhaps only a few minutes would have been enough, and we would have grasped the origin of birth."

A flurry of activity sets in. Remu is bringing the cradle; Martina anxiously follows him. Confusedly I move to and fro. Everywhere I trip over something or someone trips over me. Everywhere something small is happening and it is as if, with this bustle, we were blowing away the whole overlong day and its black sun, stream murmuring in the glen, darkling plain. At the last it is as if we were blowing away even the quiet that alone allows a glimpse beneath the surface of things, and even the immobility through which the direction can be grasped. As if we ourselves—voluntarily—were setting out on the road to ruin without first having understood its meaning.

All of a sudden I find myself face to face with Martina. For a moment we are together: Remu is tending the sheep and the third has most likely lain down. We are together by her bed. There is little light here, but even so I can make out a familiar face. "Perhaps you may remember me," I force gentle words from myself. But Martina doesn't notice me. "We two," I try even more gently, "we have, I think, already met." Martina looks at me with absent eyes and drops them once again. Despite this I cannot rid myself of the feeling that she knows who I am and who she herself once was. As we stand close to each other, I feel growing in me an embarrassment linked to awkwardness. "So I . . . ," I stutter unnecessarily, "so I'm just going."

I take a few steps, but the awkwardness remains. I sit down by the fire and it flickers forlornly. The flames are already smaller and red in color. The cooling coals are singing.

At last I lie down like the others. Then, looking through the immobile surface of the darkness I try to believe that I am still myself. Born in Prague, studied in Prague, employed in Prague, domiciled in Prague. I, who on Christmas morning left bed and house and set out through streets empty of people to the station. Those were the first moments and memories of them are like dead birds whose limp bodies fly above a yawning precipice. And yet, when I count, less than six days have passed between then and now. I try to catch at least one, any one. But how can a day be grasped when it is a wound so wide that it seems to have no shores? I press six shoreless wounds, hot wounds to my body. Surely they could have been shallower, narrower. But these are mine and against all logic this fills me with gratitude. It is like a preparation for a rare, heavy gift that a man may accept if he is opened and inflamed. So what is the point of fathoming further what ought to be and what is not? A prophetic sun went down and a circular radiance touched Remu's head as he rejoiced on the white snow. And already it is the night before the seventh day, everything contracts irrevocably and Remu, all unknowing, sleeps. I lie stretched out on the inhospitable earth, perhaps I should do something, somehow fend off the march of time that impels me like a splinter forever forward. But the noose of the story binds my feet: the rope scrapes and the blisters on my heels burn. And I am still myself, the man who was once small. Who could understand it?

IV

I wake up at three o'clock at night, my tongue glued to the roof of my mouth. I go and urinate. The candles by the barrier are still burning. A weak light illuminates Martina and Remu. These two are not lying side by side but one behind the other. Martina is completely covered up. Remu sticks out his right hand from under the blanket and grips an ax on his breast. In his shepherd's face almost nothing can be seen but black tufts of beard. Martina breathes softly and a lock of her hair falls across her mouth.

"Thank you for coming as far as here," whispers my springing consciousness.

"Thank you," I agree and in contrast to the two sleepers I hardly breathe. One candle is beginning to melt, the flame flickers in alarm and Martina smiles as if in a tender dream. It is a dream of two wolfcubs who came into the world and ever since, night after night, have been huddling at their mother's body.

Remu isn't smiling and most likely never dreams. But now he is perhaps dreaming that someone is standing dangerously close and scrutinizing him.

"Thank you," it compels me to say once more, "thank you, because you were here before me and you are eternal. And you could not choose a better kingdom for yourselves. And this makes me beg the more that the misfortune I feel approaching will not touch this place, whose remoteness is so fragile and at the same time elevating that I would almost yearn to stay if I did not, as alas I know, have to aim still further on the journey at whose end there stands not you, but I myself and my meeting with myself, with her. I did not come, that is, of your will; it was the will to doubt and hesitantly follow the destiny whose inseparable part always was and will be a mystery. And only thanks to that mystery could I stand by the outline of your trail and from its imprint drink of something that I would call springing grace."

The first candle has gone out and the flame of the second is guttering. Martina vanishes in darkness; I can still see Remu and the empty cradle and I smell the sheep-barn stench that hangs above them without touching them. "May misfortune pass them by." But the second candle also goes out and it is the thirty-first of December, still the month of the longest nights and of births hidden from the world. I feel strength but at the same time the necessity to be, just at this moment, with someone who is near to me. And so I blindly run out the door to call Livie with my glued lips—thirsting.

But the landscape outside protrudes without life and freezing night has drowned the mountain valleys. The sky, against all expectation, is veiled. Only a few stars flicker like dimmed speckles with the waning disk of the moon. I stand on the edge of the trampled area, behind me the chalet and below my feet the glen—the enormous baking dish of the mountains at whose bottom water murmurs into the gates of the universe—incommensurable with time, incommensurable with the longings of humankind.

"So call her! Call your Livie!"

No, I cannot. And yet I feel her in the air. It is she, but it is also the mountain spruce with the green-blue lichen on its sweet-smelling bark; it is the proximity of wolves. I wait for one of them to appear. I even look upward to see if I can't make out a wolf body flashing there somewhere among the stars, and it really seems to me that the sky a little way from the moon is more than black; it seems to me that I can see the arched back of a dim black shape.

I turn back to the chalet and it appears unexpectedly close to me. May purity protect it. What if I brought an infection—not good enough to smooth over the trail against the forces of worldly evil? What if I am a mere tool? An abortive sage who goes after a voice, but misses some words, understands others only in part and fails to rid yet others of the silting dust. What if I become an unwilling bearer of bacilli, a soulless bridge that aims toward the right bank yet allows anyone to cross who wants to cross?

The chalet is silent. Behind it and around it is the slope. Nowhere any omen, just the fragile chalet amid the white plump slope.

V

A shaggy bundle licked my nose. At the threshold of the seventh day I looked into guileless eyes. But already Martina was here and moved it where supposedly it would be safe. Outside dawn had broken only in part. I remembered the morning of the naked day when I had awakened alone on the carpet between the bookcase and the table. That banished morning when objects marched above me and pond water splashed somewhere in the half-dark of the overfilled room. The morning when under the weight of approaching events we had not come together.

Detached, I now watch the bustling Martina. Her still girlish hips stand out clearly under red knitwear. The wolfcubs hungrily whine. Remu takes out the dung. "Life is like a duckpond on the village green," it struck me, "and I'm stuck on its banks."

I am stuck on an ugly, trampled bank. It is beyond all doubt that I will have to go still further, and because I don't know when, why, or where, I am filled with a kind of moving equanimity. Again I belong to myself, to my own fate, however impenetrable. "And I belong to it with you," says my springing consciousness.

I am stumbling above the unchanged scenery of the valley. "Oho," Remu greets me, chopping wood. He straightens up from his hard labor and gives a thumbs-up sign: "Buna?"

No, I am unable to smile. The mountains at that hour look bewitched; on the slopes, the remnants of night are still swaying. "Such hopelessness," it occurs to me. I have to lean on the doorframe. As in a dream the cords of trodden paths are flashing in front of me. Of these the first, the one by which we came, twists directly toward the stream. The second ends in a heap of manure, and the third aims downward and far away, to the upper edge of the woods. I dwell on this last path with unthinking wonder. Remu notices it, points to the logs, his back, and the path. The sight of him fills me with comradeship and gratitude. It's not difficult to imagine the trust with which the falling trees give themselves up to him in the forest. With the same trust Martina too would surely fall if he decided to cut the feet from under her. With the same trust anyone would fall, and only Livie would utter a quiet no, but before she spoke the tender moisture would rise to her eyes.

The light increases, and remnants of mist quickly disappear from the pale blue sky. Remu occasionally straightens up from his work and these are the moments when the last of the three paths seems to run right up into his head. It reminds me of the small black radiance that yesterday flew up to it in his moment of joy. Now that radiance spilled out through the mountains and made them unfriendly.

The fire blazes up and the blissful solitude of mother Martina no longer surprises me. Even the fact that the third is packing with absurd but iron logic; even this doesn't surprise me. It is only that a chill breathes on me from his preparations. But the place where I would warm myself no longer exists. The chalet looks like a gypsy encampment, the sheep behind the barrier press together by the water; the trough has frozen during the night and the sheep bleat plaintively. The wolfcubs scrabble out of the cradle, and Martina lovingly picks them up and returns them one after the other and does so again and again, with unending patience. Remu comes up, climbs over the fence, breaks the ice, throws a fistful of salt into the trough. His boots are covered with dung and I cannot understand how it was possible that he didn't smell of it that time in the train compartment.

The third has packed up and is ready for departure. The sheep slurp. Remu has dug out some cheese somewhere and wants to give it to Martina, but she is already giving suck again. "A morning for lunacy," I think, and I feel that perhaps the way these two live together here does not even belong to the world. Feelings of listlessness, exhaustion, and chill mingle inside me with a longing to be somehow present in their relationship. And yet I know that I ought to pack, as the third has done.

The sun climbed up above the summits; the mountains became transparent and opened under the stroke of the rays.

The sun ascended and today was rosily guileless—gone was the foreboding of the last days. The event prophesied was yet to come, but life up there had already returned to its normal course. On the saddle from which we had come yesterday, a deep shadow still lay, but here in front of the chalet the snow lightened, little sparkles peeped out and it seemed to me that through them a being tender and close was watching me. "I know," I whispered, "and it doesn't surprise me that you are so very near. Not even that time, when we returned from your attic and you lay in my sleeping bag (pale, defenseless, trembling) were you as near to me as now."

I squatted down to my tired feet, and so the sparkles dulled and dissolved, and when I bent forward, thousands of ice crystals stretched their bony hands toward me. Someone stood at my back: it was Martina with the wolfcubs in her arms, and far below us, in the place where the track opened from the forest onto the naked plateau, appeared a squad of bailiffs.

"So it's here," breathed my springing consciousness and the mountains stood aghast at their own powerlessness. By some chance Remu had just come out in front of the door and behind him the third. We all stood on the flat space as if on some ice floe, the sun shone and the floe carried us into the blue-yellow sky.

It was already possible to see that the squad was made up of three men in black overcoats and one wolf. I looked at Martina to see what she would say to it. But Martina was smiling at the way the wolfcubs were squabbling—she lived even now by her one care. Even Remu looked in no way dejected, he had put his ax away somewhere and with his hands in his pockets he was hanging about near Martina. I realized that anyway nothing could be done and that this was right, because no force and no barbed wire could be permitted to protect fragile places. Anybody must be permitted to come, and whatever his intention, the distance would only open itself out into the journey like a dazzling white carpet. The distance opened in faith.

The men had drawn closer to a distance of some five hundred meters, and the wolf trotted to their right in the untrodden snow. My eyes wandered to broad-shouldered Remu. He sensed my gaze and calmly, in explanation, said: "Fratele meu."

The commando made rapid progress, the sun went on shining, the landscape opened its legs in resignation, and the stream murmured in step. The men had now got over the last ascent and appeared a few hundred meters from us along the slope. At the back walked Lanky, in the middle the chief with the cat face; the wolf trotted a little way off with head hung down. But I was most interested in the man who came first. It was Romu. Yes, once again he. He who had emerged from no-man's-land so that later he could throttle me in the corridor and later still become the custodian of all my deeds, a power arising from the shadows and at the same time a chieftain, the commander of trespass—truly a murderer—the murderer Romu. He walked first, on his head a lambskin cap and wearing the same overcoat as every second person here. Even at this distance I felt his body, which water had not touched.

The last few meters. Remu stepped forward onto the mouth of the path as if he wanted to welcome guests. It was truly so, he welcomed guests. But above the valley spread Romu's imperious voice. Romu angrily gesticulated: it concerned Remu, the chalet, maybe even Martina. It seemed not to concern me.

Remu answered in his own fashion, half joking and half

serious; it was amazing to observe these two standing face to face—roughly the same size, roughly the same age, roughly with the same strength and at the same time so different, so intensely mutually contradictory while yet something incomparably deeper flowed between them, something primeval in foundation, something that usually has no place in the relationship of people so eternally alien to each other.

The chief and Lanky looked at him indifferently, then at me, at Martina, at the chalet and again at Remu and Martina. The wolf also bided its time. I would have thought that it would in some way have reacted to the presence of the wolfcubs but it simply stood, eyes extinguished; they had extinguished his wolf's face, and it was as if the soul of a beast had not been concealed behind it for a long time. I thought: "You are not a wolf—they have taken the individuality of a living creature—they have taken you from yourself."

The wolfcubs began to moan; perhaps they had a foreboding. Martina wrapped them in a scarf and Romu raised his voice almost to insanity. It seemed he was reproaching Remu for something. And Martina stood: straight black hair fell around her face to below her breast. Here in the empty space she was not so tall; it had been an impression produced by the self-confident proportions of her body.

And then it happened: Romu took a step forward. He was more and more aggressive and it looked as if at any moment he would assault Remu. Then Remu with a playful gesture grasped Romu's cap and put it on his own head. His laughter sounded in my ears like the swish of a scythe.

Romu for a fragment of a moment stiffened. Then his hand fell like lightning to his belt and a shot rang out. Only one shot. Remu fell and went on smiling. Only when he hit the ground was his smile extinguished. The snow colored with blood.

Romu now stood without his cap, wordless, alone. With the barrel of the pistol he still aimed into space, and depression from the deed committed drifted down on him like a flock of birds of prey. But Remu, he who had been the wisest among us, had already ceased to breathe.

"Do what you have to do," Romu commanded. Even from his insensate figure it was perceptible that something had happened here too serious for it to slip off him leaving no trace. And if he had the feeling that once again he had fulfilled his role, then this time he did not do so gladly, from his heart.

But already his assistants were at hand, self-confident and cruel. Lanky dashed toward Martina, who from the moment that the gun had fired had stood like a statue. She did not defend herself even when he tore from her both wolfcubs and threw them onto the plump snow. The chief made for the door of the chalet, from which the third was emerging with his pack on his back. The chief shouted, at which the wolf took off and jumped through the open door. For an instant there was silence, and then the heart-rending bleating of the sheep. The wolfcubs also wailed and comically tried to scrabble out of the cold white substance in which they had sunk up to their bellies. These hairy little creatures had never before known anything but their mother's breast, their mother's care. The first to pay for it was the sturdier of the two; he had already almost fought through to the trodden-down area when Lanky kicked him with all his strength. He flew like a hopelessly burst ball and Lanky, whom I had hated from the first moment, moved toward the other—still unluckier, still weaker—and in the most disgusting way stamped on his head. I felt as if I were going to be sick, the more so because Martina kept on standing and watching—prepared for everything, reconciled to everything, almost too well aware of the transience of that which had only been entrusted to her—not even once lifting her eyes, or stretching out her hand in the defense of her line.

Lanky straightened himself and glanced at me with small eyes set in an asymmetrical head. With complete clarity I realized that I wouldn't take this—certainly not from him. But he had finished his job.

Everything took place with a kind of simple, self-evident inexorability that did not exceed the framework of the command. The destroyers walked here and there. They obviously wanted to leave as soon as possible; the third waited with his pack on his back and not even Martina looked as though she would resist a final departure. The sun rose into the ever clearer sky and cold rays fell down on us; one wolfcub lay deformed in front of me, the other's spine protruded a little way off, and by the mouth of the path, with a dark cap on his head, cooled the body of Remu. There was absolute silence; only from the interior of the chalet came the bleating of sheep and the racket of gunfire.

The space became desolate and the building deteriorated before my eyes. Gone were the moments when the wolfcubs had played in it, when Remu had made the fire, tended the sheep, and chopped wood, and smiled like a fox when Martina—full of grace—had nourished her two bundles from inexhaustible springs of love. Birth—the strange blessing of that place—had been ruined.

THE TOUCH OF SNOW

I

I REMAINED IN FRONT OF THE CHALET, ALONE. BELOW, ON THE path leading to the forest, all those departing were still visible: the bailiffs, Martina, the third, . . . and me. My figure was unexpectedly small and bent among the others. I couldn't help being moved: "So this . . . , this then am I."

I felt like waving, somehow expressing myself, somehow arousing the attention of those below. But the men and the one woman did not look back. Like actors after the performance they were returning to their worldly fates. First again went Romu, but his otherwise self-confident figure was unusually feeble, abject. Immediately after him, with the blue pack on his back, strode the third contentedly. Lanky followed. I recognized myself by the poles and knitted hat with the pompom. The little group, from which the wolf was surprisingly missing, ended with the chief with the cat face. Or rather it ended with a several-meter gap, beyond which Martina stumbled over a naked plateau that looked untrodden: Martina pulled her feet out heavily and sank them again, and only occasionally, maybe only when she found a footprint, stepped forward faster. But immediately behind her calves the plateau smoothed over completely and with final effect.

I sat down on a log, the group below stretched out and

slowly approached the forest. Now only two blind pathways led away from me; I was surrounded by a kingdom of snow. While the little figures grew smaller, I began to realize that here no living person existed for me. Remu's body lay as before and the corpses of the wolfcubs began to resemble indecent freaks of nature, whose intimate organs had been afflicted by malignant disease. Those responsible for it had already become mere specks barely visible to the eye. It seemed to me that one speck, perhaps that one with the bobble hat on its head, remained standing on the edge of the forest whose shadow had already swallowed the others. Then even that speck vanished and the mountains became silent. My wedding with Livie began.

Perhaps five, perhaps ten minutes of solitude passed. Nothing moved, only the sun continued in its journey over the crystal-white mountains. Hesitantly I stood up and approached the prostrate Remu. He was curled on his side and was smiling slightly. I took another step. Never before had I found myself in such proximity to a corpse. His thick black beard gave the impression that I had before me a wax figure stuck together from individual parts. (If I pulled at them, they would certainly come loose.) And yet it was still him—my friend Remu. The fact that he would no longer move, grimace, open his eyes, was absurd.

"So you see this is how you have ended, Remu, and you too ended like this, Simeonu Cudeanu, when they used batons against you." As I stood above the huddled body it seemed to me that far below it I could see Livie and Simeonu in companionable conversation. "Could you think of giving her to me?" it struck me. "I know that you had a deep relationship. But you ought to take more care of your Mirela. She has remained alone in your flat. (Once you made love there.) Who will help her if not you?"

As if to the bottom of the ocean I sank down into my solitude and it brought me not anxiety but contentment.

The blood under Remu's body had at first soaked into a part of the snow and then had frozen. I lost consciousness of the whole and saw in it an expression of a desolation that assails. My heart opened and the snow colored with more and more blood. The steam stank of iron, but it was not that I wanted to lose something; I wished only to make up the difference, as if the universe had become my artificial organ.

At last I walked toward the chalet. I could hear my steps. Steps, steps. Inside everything was as it had been. I found myself by the barrier at the back. Here, in the half-darkness mingled with strips of light lay the herd of sheep. Individual sheep had fallen with torn out throats or lungs shot through, or both. Lying across their bodies here was the wolf too, with two gunshots in its chest. In that instant I followed its entire journey here from below, and its tragedy, the tragedy of a creature robbed of soul, struck me as the greatest of all.

For a moment I looked at the bloody wolf's teeth. The chalet aged by another year. "Leave!" said my springing consciousness.

I took my pack and went out. But what a change this revealed: no longer (even a blind) path, no trodden-down space. My feet were gripped by cold, glittering fetters. From a drift not far away protruded Remu's coat, cap, hair. The wrecked skeleton of the chalet was silent.

"I am always only leaving ruined places," I said.

"You are always only drawing closer to the final victory," said my springing consciousness.

I took one last look at the edge of the forest, perhaps to convince myself that everybody had by now truly vanished. With absent eyes I scanned the highlands, only now emerging from the haze. Then I turned to the opposite side where the December sun flamed above the white heads of the summits. Its rays fell right to the bottom of the glen. I took a few heavy paces. Simply for myself I had to laugh out loud when I remembered those who had departed. I walked round the ruins of the building. In that moment I was suffused with a strange unreal warmth; she whom I had betrayed caressed me, and I discovered with emotion that the universe—the artificial organ of us all—had her likeness and she its likeness. I set off up the silent slope.

II

Our caravan went down through the woods to the stream. On its foamy surface the sun fell through the gaps in the treetops. Depressed, I raised my feet, somewhere inside myself I stood still, and yet I couldn't help moving. My mind kept on starting with the image of my last sight of the plateau: the ransacked chalet loomed black over the glen, and despite the fact that almost nothing could be made out against the sun, I knew that he who was sitting in front of it was myself. It was already very distant; I felt rather than being able to see my body, hands, feet, and bobble hat. "What if I stayed, returned to myself up there?" the thought occurred to me at one point. But the trail behind had vanished; Martina was already only stepping into individual craters of footprints; and further on, behind her back, untrodden space reestablished itself. Nobody could manage to go back in these circumstances. "So adieu then, you whom I have left here forever, coward that I am." The stream murmured, Lanky panted and from the other side thumped the chief's feet. Romu always kept up the same tempo, nobody said anything, nobody seemed to be compelling me to anything, and it ceased to be clear to me whether I was going with them voluntarily or under the threat of force. "What I'd like best would be to kick you into the current and watch your black, vaseline-soaked overcoats floating!"

As we went on, the route changed in a familiar way. The spruces thinned out and grew bigger, the snow decreased and was not so pure. "Break," gestured Romu. It was in the ravine above a frozen pool. All the bailiffs lit up; we stood about in the forest dimness and the clear day swam somewhere above us. The third winked at me, and when I only shrugged my shoulders, he pretended that he understood me. But I still hadn't managed to grasp what had happened up there. Even now Romu looked not quite himself; he stood there silently, while his assistants forced out hoarse words. Since he had interrogated me in the Restaurant Europa the chief with the cat face had grown a thick beard; the image that I had assigned to him in my mind had already ceased to suit him. Meanwhile Lanky was still the same abortive person. A man with a rhomboid head.

Between the trees emerged Martina. Her red woolen garment was heavy and soaked at the hem. Very slowly, unrelated to anything, she came closer. But the bailiffs would wait no longer. From the fact that they were indifferent to her I understood that they were also indifferent to me. I felt terribly cheated: "What then was it all for? Why the interrogations, threats, pursuit?" Nothing remained but to admit that I had been a mere pawn in a game that was immeasurably greater. Or even worse: really a self-proclaimed wise man who had set off after a voice, but had missed some words, had understood others only in part . . .

Martina neither increased nor slowed her pace and maybe didn't even see us. I remembered her as a girl whose soul barred her from the lot of a woman; she too surely remembered it. Now she had lost the last and only chance she had been given. What is more, this chance had taken the form of two innocent wolfcubs who had loved her.

I remained standing by the frozen pool until I found myself somewhere in the middle between those men and her. An unending white veil was approaching from above. Martina was swimming on its edge, vanishing and again emerging; the veil slipped through the spruce copse, and only a few moments were left before it would swallow me. I realized that those men were now truly mine, that I depended on them. As fast as I could I set out after them.

The valley had widened, and there was much less snow. The veil lay above the bubbling surface of the stream. "So I am back down," I thought, "down again on earth." The future lay before me like a dead stinking sea. Its lack of direction was terrifying.

We came out where the road began and here two jeeps were standing. The silence above them had the intensity of gunfire. I saw how the distance between me and Livie was irrevocably expanding: "Can it really be possible that we shall never meet again? Is it possible that it will remain forever without an end, what we lived through together?"

The bailiffs were smoking again, and as if they sensed what I was thinking they partly encircled me. The third shed his pack and breathed in appreciatively. We were now only waiting for Martina. But she was not in sight, even though here the trees did not obscure the view. The sun had reached its summit and was now sinking behind the wooded slopes. I leaned on the frame of the driver's cabin.

Immediately Martina appeared Romu opened the door and Lanky did the same at the second car. I got in against my will but voluntarily, seeing that there was no other solution. It was the same as the moment when I had set off into the fields. Then it had been completely dark; the asphalt had scratched; in front of me I had had an empty road, behind me the State of Emergency and the unfortunate apparition of Mirela. All this came back to my mind before I sat down. A deep narrow crack had formed closely below the running board. My feet flapped briefly above it. Somebody kicked at the door from outside; someone else made a comment at the expense of the lagging Martina. Through the back glass I saw the trail by which she had come. We also had walked it. Those few footprints in the snow, this was indeed the last place where the past still lived. But the trail shortened with each step that Martina took. And when Martina had arrived, there was no trail, there were only mountains.

I felt myself becoming my own conscience, a cotenant of the creator's garment on the shoulder of the rounded ridges. The landscape broadened out and became one, its integrity broken only by my shadow reaching deeply downward. My tongue was glued to the roof of my mouth, my shoulders sore from the straps and my boots full of snow. More was falling into them, but it was as if this was happening somewhere apart, far away, and maybe even long ago. My head was spinning. Everything that I had experienced in the last seven days was coalescing in it.

I climbed several dozen meters and set off straight ahead. Noon went by and the sun began to drop. It warmed. The weaker I became the better I walked. From the far distance there floated to me the scent of bark. It was dawning on me that I was aiming toward the place where I had always aimed, that is to places where from the ice-covered plateau grew the mountain spruce, the one with green-blue lichen on its sweet-smelling bark. Suddenly I felt my hand rapidly turning to wood—stiffening. I was suffused with an inexpressible happiness, the happiness of the knowledge that nobody and nothing could any longer stand between me and her. In that moment of enlightenment I was proud of myself. Yes, proud: I had not sold out to skepticism or cynicism, and armed with the will to listen to the inner voice I had overturned the logic of lead and iron batons. Behold, the gates are opening. "Thank you for allowing me to pass into the light of your grace, as well as through the darkness of your absence and the grayness of human vanity. You have seen that everything which I have experienced from birth until the departure of one train from one Prague station was no more than a single day. Thank you that I too have seen it. You have seen that I yearned for an encounter through which I could conclude this eternal agreement. Thank you that I too have seen it. Thank you for her name, which I pronounced for so short a time, and yet in doing so my every cell trembles. I know that it is folly to found my actions on a single fleeting relationship. I know how dubious is every retrospective judgment. Why, no more than a few hours could have passed and we might ourselves have parted, voluntarily. . . . Only I also know how her hand held on to mine in the mounting pressure of bodies. I recall the coolness of her fingers wordlessly clenched. And brown eyes, startled eyes, I remember, and this is just that word that cannot be painted over or wiped from the gate of eternity or uprooted from one's own heart . . . for the last station of these eyes, that station in time when neither of us thought of parting, belonged to me."

At this my hand had already changed into a coniferous tree: the joints were paralyzed, the sleeve had burst under the thrust of branches. Irrevocably one body we went on. And with every step the palm of the other hand flowed outward and back, until it resembled a rock and ice alternating in the same measure as I had seen them at the beginning of the mountains. I perceived these metamorphoses only slightly although they brought me pleasure. I kept on always in the same direction; the sky somewhere above me blackened and dropped down, creating a low belt. I found myself at the beginning of a frozen lake. The basin around me resembled a plate from whose sides a red-white radiance flowed down toward the center. Across the snow-covered surface two people drew closer to each other: Andrei and I. Andrei stumbled, dragging his feet, and yet it looked as if he was not walking but floating—propelled by the strokes of an invisible paddle. I started to feel uncomfortable that my hand-tree stuck out into his path like a bar. But it stuck from the right and it was soon clear that we would miss each other by some ten meters to the left. The distance between us was slowly diminishing.

We met in the focus of the entire basin—in the middle of the lake. I saw Andrei's hand in its sling and his feverishly burning eyes. The disrespect with which he had reacted to me from the very beginning was still there even now, even when exhaustion and my undoubted perseverence made him more approachable. We didn't even have to open our mouths—even without them we pronounced her name.

"Is she alive?" I croaked, without recognizing my own voice.

"I don't know," he said, and the despair he nevertheless did not wish to share with me remained on his lips.

As we stood opposite each other, the tracks we each had made led from the far distance up to this spot and anyone who didn't understand the curse of parallel lines might have thought we had been journeying toward each other.

"You have no news of her?" I tried again.

"None."

I noticed that he gazed suspiciously at my transmuted hands. (Perhaps he still does not want to believe that I am serious in my intention.) For me this part of his character was repellent. We were silent. He had the same narrow nose as Livie. His face was swollen, full of scratches. I remembered that exciting night when I had admired his will. The morning had then brought a rupture between brother and sister, after which he had left and I had entered the forlorn kitchen.

While I was thus meditating, the white plain shone bewitchingly before me. "I am waiting for your steps," it said.

"I'm just coming," I said and I did so. Behind my back I left my own fellow pilgrim through this unearthly land— Livie's brother Andrei.

The mouth of the basin was hemmed by a series of rounded forms. As I saw black, blue, and white, I couldn't make out whether they were boulders, wolves, or simply other colored phantoms. The snow here was deep and powdery and Andrei's footprints led at ever the same distance from me. I thought: when he got through, so must I. I raised my head a little and here I saw my father standing on the other side of a snowdrift. He looked reproachful and said: "Don't think that one short moment can decide whether you are a good man!" (These were words that he had already once thrown in my face.) But when I looked back at my story, good and evil were disappearing one into the other. And so I realized that home and parents, the Christmas tree, and the unfinished cakes were terribly distant and that all that repeated itself every year with a million variations was a mere reflection, a kind of fossilized form of that which here (in the time into which I had entered) was still materializing.

The drift remained behind me. Andrei's footsteps veered to the side and my transformed being grew. Something forced me to smile. What a strange blessing, what a proof of belonging to all and everything: to have ice, rock, and tree erupting in my body.

IV

Behind the smudged window flashed the flat, gray landscape. The snow had vanished together with the forests and the blackfrost could bite at will into the exposed meadows and fields. The sun neared the horizon, from which it glittered through a ring of New Year's Eve haze.

Slowly we passed a convoy of military vehicles. The drivers one after the other pulled their great vans toward the edge. At the gates of a church several grandmothers remained standing. Otherwise the villages looked as if they had died out.

Finally the road in front of us cleared and both cars leaped forward. In the first were only the chief and Romu. Ours was driven by Lanky, with Martina next to him, and in the back I and the third—in our laps our packs. My pack was touching my chest in which dwelt my worn-out heart. We negotiated a bend and for a moment I watched the exhaust fumes of the cars mingling above a meadow. "If I could only walk the land out there again. Let the coolness of the falling mist refresh me. Walk the uneven lanes. Just once more be close to myself and so to Livie."

Lanky drove doggedly, with a cynical contempt. We kept on driving at the same speed, the highest the road allowed. The third tried to tell me something, but I didn't feel like listening to his in any case incomprehensible words. It came to me that he was desecrating the knowing silence of Martina, who shared with us a place so unbecoming for her— blessed among women. If I had stretched out my hand, I could have grasped her hair. But I felt that even then I would have been no closer to her because the distance between us there inside was measured not in meters but in the kilograms that weighed our fates.

"What should I do then? Watch myself watching and letting myself be driven? Scrutinize, with a spectator's patience, how it hurts?"

For some time we had already been driving through a village festooned with countless slogans. The letters flashed by and provoked a chain of memories. The mist started to thicken. Before us appeared a station.

"Time does not run slower at the end," I realized. "You are already past the door the moment you enter the door."

The brakes screamed, the door-hinges of the first car clicked. "Out!" said Lanky—he who had murdered both Martina's offspring. They pulled the door ajar. I saw the chief and Romu. Behind them stretched a space empty of people but for me already forbidden. "Who will stand in the way I do not wish to take? Who will derail me?"

For an instant we all stood in confusion, and so it was not apparent who was the defeated and who the victor. The chief and Lanky waited to see what Romu would do, and he buttoned his overcoat. The third paced up and down. Martina stared at the ground and I don't know why I had a vision of a slaughterhouse gate and a contented, tail-waving cow.

As we walked through the waiting room it still seemed to me that I had plenty of time. Behind the counter a small light shone and under my feet crackled the dust—that sad blood of this Country. The bailiffs behaved to us with distaste, condescendingly. We turned to the right and went out onto the platform. Again, still time. But at that moment I saw the train ready for departure and I understood everything: "I will never again see my Livie."

My heart pounded in confused anxiety. The green wagons stood on the fourth, last track. "What if she really is somewhere? Without news, without certainty, left only with the faith that I will not leave it like this, gazing into the growing evening, with the objects surrounding her ungraspable, just like her hope that dies, and is again born, faltering. "So where are you then? I feel your proximity and pain; even your efforts to recall my face. . . . But instead you remember only the touch of my hand, that touch with which you will grow old and afterward lose certainty whether the man still lives who touched you."

We crossed the tracks, the iron doors creaked. The first to slide into the empty carriage was the third. "Hurry!" shouted Lanky, who probably wanted us to know that he did not intend to spend New Year's Eve in a godforsaken station. I swung myself up the steps, and even before me Martina obeyed the command with the fluid movements of a machine. The bailiffs below still gaped at us. I wanted to turn round and ask, "Why, really?" but the door window was painted white and the corridor was on the other side.

A new environment surrounded me. The third made himself comfortable in the first compartment, Martina remained standing at the beginning of the corridor and it was as if a sealed diaphragm stretched around her. The car jerked, started up, and after a moment was already moving with remarkable speed. Behind the windows flashed houses, sheds, trees. Inside it was cold and the dark kept thickening. With the pack on my back I walked through to the other end of the corridor. The padlock here prevented passage to the next wagon. I remained there standing helplessly. The shadows were breaking and falling onto the Formica panels. "When it stops somewhere, I must try to get off," it occurred to me. But I knew that this was a train that does not stop.

V

The sun dropped, its last rays were swinging over the edges of protrusions. The warmth of a girl's body floated toward me from an illuminated bed.

The space flattened out completely; it was only my height now and my hands struck into it and touched the low sky. My right foot turned into the barrel of a rifle and sank into the hardened snow. But the left foot became a wolf's paw and with unbelievable ease slid over the fragile surface. On the horizon (I had long ago lost any idea whether it was one meter, ten meters or a kilometer away) small groups of four-legged spots formed. They moved. Truly like a blue-white bed the highland landscape encircled me. "No, I don't have to say good-bye to you, smallness, which binds human hearts in a harness of well-trodden approaches. Not even to you, modern inertia, which prevents man from grasping seriously the message of his inner voice. You have vanished, as streets, stations, houses have vanished from me; as has vanished the half-dark of all apartments through which I ever passed in my life back there (that intimate half-dark of ever identical corridors, bathrooms, rooms)."

I found myself on a traverse where everything either ascended or descended. The black spots now dared to come closer and closer. Their shaggy bodies I perceived by touch.

It was growing late, and I dedicated all my efforts to preventing the strange compound that I had become from coming to a halt. But I didn't hurry and I wasn't afraid. It didn't matter whether it was day or night, winter or summer. Anything that does not last forever here lost significance. The scent of the mountain spruce—that which stood before me and within me throughout that time—flooded the air and with every movement thickened. Frost stabbed into my eyes, ice crystals forming on my lips.

We approached the altar: I and the girl. She wore the fur coat in which I had seen her for the first time. Now, when I knew her inside and out, she smiled just as shyly; only the features of her face were painfully clenched under the surface.

"I am so glad that you have come, Martin."

But the altar began to withdraw, as if it wished to lead us somewhere. I took her with the utmost care around the shoulders and we set forth. She resembled a cloud of mist—she flowed alongside me, changed in density, vanishing. "Remu is dead," I thought, "the wolfcubs have perished, I know nothing of your father, and yet have the feeling that I am where I should be. Many things have encroached on me, and I have seen much cruelty. And now I have returned to you, so that through you I can step out of the bondage of time, although it would never have occurred to me before. Such is your Country, the living body for him who seeks direction. I came here because I could do no other, Livie."

I proceeded at her side and the burden of tiredness that always comes after battle was throwing me, despite all closeness, into loneliness. Now, when she was beside me, when the muzzles of wolves were touching our bodies, when all these complicated and long events through which I had passed had issued into this thread of peace, I could allow myself to remain myself, to savor our union as a mere possibility that could, however, be entered whenever I wanted. But suddenly my surroundings grew bright; I saw the glittering wedges of mountains, even the forests in the distance;

my gaze slid along the rugged crests down into the basin and again back upward and nowhere here was there a living creature—not even a sign of one, even the wolves were not here. I was completely alone, and even more: I stood in the middle of the slope. Again I looked round at the nearest places. Only the rigid edges of the boulders interrupted the integrity of the white field. "It's nothing," I said to myself. "She has hidden herself from me and is waiting ahead—my wanton Livie." In trust I took a step, a second, a third. The drop was so sheer that the wolf's paw started to slip; I was now leaning only on the rifle barrel and even that was failing to hold. It was impossible to go up or down. In front of me a totally windswept strip, and although the sun had just gone down, its surface had a silver-gray sheen.

"You won't catch me or deter me."

Determined, I lunged out to attack. In that moment my foot slipped, the second fell from its hold and my whole body helplessly flapped in the air. By then I was already hurtling with growing speed to a destination unknown and I tried in vain to put together fragments of thought, whose parts and even mere flashes remained behind. I realized only this much—that I would not manage to answer the question of what had caused this slide. Then came a somersault, a second, followed by a flight with arms outstretched, a blow to the head, darkness. A blow to the neck.

I opened my eyes and among colored pots I saw a strange phenomenon: from the ground on which I lay grew a marvelous spruce whose branches were peacefully stretching above me and were bringing me closer to the darkening sky. The trunk was overgrown with lichen; it compelled me to embrace it closely, at least with my gaze. From places that I could not see I heard a wolf purring. One wolf—it was he who had already once wanted to share my cross—appeared by me and tenderly licked my face. "I know you," I tried to tell him with my eyes. "You are a very good wolf, perhaps the best of all wolves."

The four-legged figure blurred; the world stumbled and spun around. With weakening eyes I watched a green veil. It became cooler. Floating like a silk scarf came Livie. My eyelids fell—there where she should have been I now saw light, elsewhere darkness. Livie took my head in her palms. When I have slept we shall go for a walk. I felt the warmth of her smile.

Then there was nothing. There was the touch of snow.